DARKEST FATE

Fabio Bueno

Booklings Publishing

Booklings Publishing

Darkest Fate
Copyright © 2014 Fabio Bueno

Cover Design by Martina Elise Dalton

First Edition, 2014

ISBN: 0985877960
ISBN-13: 978-0-9858779-6-5

To

Elza

Chapter 1: Drake

I've lost everything.

Today has been a whirlwind. Skye, my now ex-girlfriend, is on the verge of being kicked out of her coven forever. Boulder was dragged away from the fingers of death. Mona almost caused another citywide calamity.

When I finally figured out I'd fallen for Skye, I messed up. I asked my little sister to use her secret magical powers to heal my best friend. Mona saved Boulder's life, but she left a trail of magical energy that other witches picked up. They still don't know that Mona is the Singularity, but it's just a matter of time. And Skye, who lied to her covens to protect my sister, was shipped to London to answer for her betrayal.

It's been the longest day of my life.

I'm driving back from the airport, still trying to regroup after Skye left. I promise myself that I will help her, no matter what. Even if she doesn't come back to me, I will make things right.

Mona is in the passenger seat, silent. No doubt she's pondering what the hectic day means for her life.

I'm eager to get home, sleep, and rest. But before that, I need some time to calm down, to breathe. The I-5 is unusually empty, even this late in the evening, so I pull over and get out of the car.

It's a cold night. The rare clear sky lets the moonlight through. I stare at the moon, at the stars. We're close enough to the airport that I can see planes taking off. One of them is taking Skye away from me.

Mona comes over and puts her hand on my shoulder. "She's gone, Drake. Let's go home."

I look at her. She's much shorter than me. She looks like a child, with her arm raised like that just to reach me. But she's not a kid anymore.

Time to forget my troubles and focus on Mona. She's the one in danger.

"Let's bounce," I tell her.

We climb inside the Volvo and resume our drive home.

"What should we do?" Mona asks me.

"Skye told me the covens will be keeping an eye on everyone connected to her. That means you and me, maybe the gang at school, and her aunt Gemma."

"Like surveillance?" Mona sounds disconcertingly calm.

"Why aren't you freaking out?" I ask.

She shrugs. "Why should I?"

I scoff. "Well, first, you almost lost control of your magic again when we were helping Boulder. Then the witch assassin attacked us. What would have happened if Jane hadn't shown up to rescue you? And now the Night covens are after you."

She taps her long purple fingernails on the dashboard. "Exactly. I know what I'm dealing with here. Except for the surveillance part that you didn't explain to me."

Mona has come such a long way since she figured out her magical powers. Sometimes I can't believe my little sister is the one uttering these words.

"Well?" she asks impatiently.

"Skye mentioned bugs and people being followed. They have no reason to suspect us, but they know Skye discovered the Singularity's identity."

"Aren't they dragging her off to London to force her to confess? Why would they follow us?"

"Because they're afraid the Night covens will find out about you before them."

She shows me the burner cell phone Jane gave me. "Is that why we're using this cell?"

"Yep. Jane says it's untraceable."

We drive in silence for a while. I-5 is eerily quiet tonight. Or maybe I'm seeing ominous signs everywhere.

"Is Boulder all right?" she asks.

"Yes! Thanks to you, Mona. Sean called me and told me Boulder is awake. He asked me to visit tomorrow, but I don't know if I should. It may attract attention to him."

"Don't you think it'll be *more* suspicious if you don't visit your best friend who just came out of a coma?"

I nod. "But what if they figure out that he woke up from a coma all of a sudden?"

"How? How would the covens know that? His parents and the nurse won't talk. I trust Yara and Pain."

I need to thank Yara too; she was the one who did the commune ritual to save Boulder. Without her, he would never have made it.

And Pain, Mona's best friend, still doesn't know that Mona is safe. "Oh, yeah, speaking of Pain. You need to let her know you're okay. But warn her about the surveillance. You can still talk to each

3

other on the phone; just don't mention anything about magic and stuff."

"I guess it means that for both of us, the best thing is do nothing, right? Go to school, see our friends, behave normally."

"We could use some normal."

She sighs. "It makes sense. Let's stop by Pain's now, then. She'll freak out if I don't talk to her soon."

I drive to Pain's house and park in the driveway. "Don't take too long. It's getting late."

Of course, Mona ignores me. I had to jump-start the car battery this afternoon when we left Boulder's house, so I leave the car running the whole time. On one hand, that's good: it's freezing outside, and I needed to keep the heat on anyway. But it costs me twenty minutes of gas.

The door opens, and Mona and Pain come out. They take their time talking on the porch. I'm trying to get my sister's attention and point to my watch, but they are hugging, oblivious to the world. Then Pain leans over Mona and kisses my sister on the lips. I mean, a *real* kiss, not a BFF one.

Huh.

It couldn't have lasted more than five seconds, but in that brief time, my train of thought almost derails. When it finally arrives at the station, the conclusion is that I should have seen that coming.

They say goodbye. Mona comes over and enters the car in a hurry, but she doesn't face me.

"Can you turn the heat all the way up?" Mona asks. "It was freezing outside." She stares blankly at Pain, who is waving at us as we leave the driveway.

After a couple of blocks, I ask, "Is that how you kids say goodbye

4

nowadays?"

Mona is still. "*She* kissed me."

"Yeah, I saw it."

Mona taps her hand against her leg. She hesitates, but says, "A while ago, I guessed that Pain liked me. But tonight she caught me by surprise."

"So are you…?"

"No. I mean, I don't know. I have no idea, really. This happened like two minutes ago. I didn't have time to process it." Mona turns to me. "But I want you to remember, I was very understanding when you came out to me." She's got an impish smile.

"Except for the fact that I've never come out to you, that's true. And you're not really coming out right now, either."

"Both good points." She slumps in the seat, looking straight ahead.

"Are you sure about this thing with Pain? I'd be careful."

"Drake, that's so unlike you."

"No, that's not what I meant." I drive slowly. It's deliberate. I want to talk about it before we get home. "What I'm worried about is that she's been your friend forever. If it doesn't work out… I hope it does work out, by the way, but if it doesn't… Please don't lose your friend."

Mona taps my hand. "I won't."

Her rare gesture of affection makes me happy. I like my little sister. She's all right. There, I said it. Or, at least, I thought it. "Also, if somebody gives you trouble in school, talk to me," I tell her.

"Oh, aren't you protective? If someone bullies me, what exactly are you going to do?"

"I don't know." I shrug. "Maybe I'll ask Boulder to do

something."

She chuckles.

When Mona and I get home, a silver Ford Focus is parked on the street. I try to remember where I've seen a car like that before.

We enter the house, and Dad rushes to receive us at the door. "Drake, Mona. Don't be alarmed. We have a visitor."

His face has an expression I've never seen before, frowning but with a glint in his eyes. A sad smile plays at the corner of his lips. Okay, that's weird.

Is it the covens? Has Skye already told them? Or maybe the Night covens figured out it's Mona. My sister and I exchange worried looks.

My father must have caught our concerned glances. "Please, don't panic. It's okay," he reassures us.

Mona and I look at each other. She says, "Dad, what's going on?"

At last, he opens the door and gestures to the living room. "Your mother is here."

It takes my brain a while to handle what he's saying. He never— ever—talks about our mother. But it's the last part of the sentence that almost knocks me out.

A short woman with big eyes and a shy demeanor enters the living room.

I recognize her from my memory. And from my old photos that burned in the house fire. And from Skye's cell phone. She's the one who was following us.

That stranger cared for me once. That tiny woman, wearing an ugly red knit sweater and faded jeans, is my mother. My mind has trouble organizing that information.

"We have a lot to talk about," she says.

"Are you kidding? We have *nothing* to talk about," Mona says.

I look at Mona. She is shaking. The physical similarities between my sister and the woman in front of us are uncanny. They have the same body type, the same round face with pale skin, the same pouty mouth. And the same flawless beauty.

This woman has Allure too. She is a witch.

Mona takes a step forward and yells at our mother, "I hate you!"

"Mona…" Dad says.

But my sister waves him off. She rushes upstairs, running up the steps as fast as she can. Her door slams shut.

Something stirs inside me. I feel nauseated, empty of energy, but full of anguish. It's like a mountain collapsed on my shoulders. This shock, after a day already full of shocks, is too much to handle.

I need to deal with it, though. No one else will.

The woman shifts her weight from one foot to another. Dad's eyes flicker from her face to mine, but her gaze is trained on me. She looks even more anxious than I feel.

I remember what Jane has told me. I straighten my spine. "Dad, can you leave us alone for a moment?"

"Buddy, are you sure?" he asks. He takes a step toward me, as if he's thinking of wrapping his arms around me. For what? Comfort? Protection? Anyway, he doesn't get any closer. But his gesture shows he's there for me.

"Please do it." I ask in a firm tone.

He looks at me and then at my mother. "Of course." He reluctantly leaves.

When I'm sure he can't hear us, I whisper, "Are you a witch?"

She sustains my stare.

"Why do you ask?" Her voice is flat.

No "what?" No surprise.

7

"If you are, you need to leave this house now and stay away from us for a while. Every second you're here, we're in danger. I can't tell you why."

She looks deep into my eyes. I make an effort to keep them calm and dry.

The woman's shoulders are not hunched anymore. Her expression becomes more relaxed. Her frown is gone. "I know why," she says softly.

"You do?" My muscles tense up. What does she mean by that?

"That's why I'm here. I know who Mona is," she whispers.

My blood freezes. "Why now? Why show up now?"

She hesitates. "I wasn't sure I should've come, but the explosion of green light today made the decision for me. I've been watching you both since the earthquake. I came here to protect her. I'd better start doing just that."

I'm at a crossroads again. I need to make a choice now. As always, I take a leap of faith.

I get a piece of paper and scribble on it. "Call me at this number. It's safe." At least, I hope it is. "We need to talk."

"Yes, we do," she replies.

My mother showed up after thirteen years. And I'm sending her away.

She makes a slight motion of trying to hug me, but I keep still. She gives up mid-movement—like Dad did a minute ago—and turns away, heading for the door. Her hand is about to touch the handle.

"Why did you leave?" I blurt out.

She faces me. Her hands tremble.

In a strained voice, she says, "I will tell you everything later. But it's not because I didn't care for you and Mona. It's precisely because

I love you both."

My mother leaves. Again. The longest day of my life just got a little longer.

She came back. But I feel more alone than ever.

Chapter 2: Skye

This is the end of my life as a Sister.

The plane lurches forward. I feel glued to the seat. As we ascend, the pressure starts to grow, compressing my lungs, not much at first, but slowly making me take deeper breaths. What's going on? I've never felt this way during a flight.

"Are you okay?" Connor asks. "Do you need anything?"

The magical signature of Connor close to me doesn't help; my body tingles with an electric current. The intensity of someone's personal magic so near is almost unbearable.

My chest tightens. I realize it's not the inertia making me hyperventilate. It's the realization that everything is crashing down around me.

"I don't want to go," I blurt out.

"You must."

"What if I don't?"

He sighs. "I'm not going to restrain you or attack you with a potion, you know that. But you made a lifetime commitment to the covens, Skye. You're beholden to it."

"Can I walk out, if I decide to do so? Wouldn't the covens send someone after me?"

"I'm sure they would, given the gravity and the urgency of the matter. But you're a responsible Sister, Skye. Your coven is officially requesting your presence. Are you going to refuse?"

As soon as the pilot turns off the seatbelt sign, I jump out of my seat and rush to the lavatory. I close the door and lean my head against it, my eyes closed, trying to control my raspy breathing.

I simply don't know how to get out of this state. I recall my meditation techniques, the same ones I use when praying and performing rituals. Thinking of the Goddess helps me for a while, but it soon reminds me that I have failed my coven. The panic comes back with a vengeance.

I turn and steady myself against the edge of the tiny sink, but that makes me face myself in the mirror. That's the last thing I need. I sit down on the closed toilet and put my head between my knees.

It helps me a little. From the seated position, I reach for the faucet, wet my hands, and dab water on my face. My cheeks feel hot. I force myself to take slow, deep breaths.

A light knock on the door is followed by Connor's voice, "Are you okay, Skye?"

"No, I'm not."

"Do you need—"

"Just go away."

I hear him talking to someone, maybe the people in line. I don't care.

My coven will question me. They'll ask me point blank who the Singularity is. I can't tell them the truth. I made a promise. But then a Mother with Truth Charm will ask me the same question, and I'll give Mona up anyway. There's no counter for Charms.

In either case, they'll banish me from the coven. I'll lose the only life I've ever known.

And Mona! How can I protect her?

My mind wanders in circles, coming back to the same dilemma over and over. I don't have a solution. I need time. I need to stall to figure out my way out of this, but also for Mona to disappear.

Another knock on the door. "Do you need help?" It's a woman's voice now.

"I'm okay. I'll be out in a few."

I use a tissue to dry my face. I still can't look in the mirror.

When I get back to the seat, Connor looks worried. "Are you sick?"

"In a manner of speaking," I say.

"It must be hard for you."

I turn to him. "If you're so concerned, let it go. Let *me* go."

He looks at me with sad eyes. "You know I can't do it, Skye. I would if I could, believe me."

I scoff. "What are you getting out of this? A promotion? A medal?"

"Come on, Skye. It's not about that." He sounds wounded. "I gave you all the credit when you found Brianna. You deserved it, and I let everyone know. Only, it was a lie."

"Are you mad I lied to you?"

"It's not that, either. You know the risks of letting the Singularity go. We all know them." He must be upset; he didn't even lower his voice when he said "Singularity."

"Ask Brianna, then. You told me they will try to wake her up from the coma."

He seems concerned. "It's not that simple. Even with our... resources, we don't know if it's possible to wake someone up from a coma."

Mona woke up Boulder by herself, I think.

Connor takes my silence as an invitation to go on. "We *do* know it's risky. It may damage her irreversibly."

"But you're going ahead anyway."

"You're making me say it aloud, aren't you?" He sighs. "I hate to tell you this, but *you* forced our hand."

"Oh, no, you're not pinning this on me. It's your doing."

"Tell us who the Singularity is, Skye." He uses a calming voice.

I shake my head. "No. You will try to wake Brianna up anyway, won't you?"

"Give us a convincing answer, and I'll see what I can do. What do you say?"

I don't reply. I just stare down the aisle.

But he asks, "Where's your phone?"

"What?"

"I know it's not on you, and it's not in your carry-on."

I turn to face him, outraged. "Did you search my stuff?"

"Don't be so righteous. You're the one in the wrong here. Where is it?"

I won't tell him, Trust Charm or not. I reset it in the town car, deleting all the data, and discreetly threw it away in a garbage can at the airport.

"Suit yourself," he says. "I won't pressure you now. I'll let you rest during the flight. But when we touch down, we'll go straight to the Mothers. And then, Goddess help you."

***

In the middle of the night, darkness takes over the plane, except for a couple of late-night readers and their courtesy lights. I can't sleep with all that's going on, and even less with Connor and all his annoying energy by my side. He can also sense my magic, but not as intensely, and he went to sleep.

A girl about my age comes out of the restroom. I consider walking to her and borrowing her phone. I've been thinking. Drake must be warned that I'll end up confessing. He needs to hide Mona.

But I know that by now, everyone who has been in contact with me will be under surveillance. I saw Connor making calls before we left. I couldn't hear him, but I'm sure that's what he was doing. Aunt Gemma, Priscilla, Drake, Yara, Greta: their home and cell phones must be tapped. Maybe Mona's too, since I dated her brother and was in her house many times. Did Aunt Gemma see me with Mona at any point? I'm not sure. I can't take the chance.

Pain! I could call Pain. They have no reason to suspect her. But her number was in my cell, and I can't remember it.

At school, I hung out with Sean and Boulder, too. Would they listen to their phones? At some point, they're bound to discover Boulder's miraculous recovery. It'd be enough to raise suspicions, and somebody may make the connection.

Speaking of Boulder's cure, how did Mona manage it? She knows the healing spell I taught her, but she couldn't have performed a healing ritual all by herself. A Sister must have helped her.

I shudder when a thought crosses my mind: did Jane help Mona cure Boulder? Even Drake wouldn't be so reckless. And Jane is wanted by the police; she wouldn't show her face in public. Her scarred face.

Who helped Mona and Drake? The only other Sisters they know are Greta and Yara. But if they helped Mona, they know she's the Singularity. If not before, then they figured it out when she released the green light. Why? Why haven't they said something to the

14

covens? What would stop a loyal Sister from sharing the most important news ever with her coven? In my case, it was concern for Mona, and in part, my affection for Drake.

I jolt in my seat. I know someone else who cares for Drake.

Yara.

I punch the armrest. Yara helped Mona to get closer to Drake. She's risking being banned, like me. For Drake. I bite my knuckles.

This will be a long trip. I wish I had a Sleep potion right now.

Chapter 3: Drake

My mother dropped by to say hello after thirteen years of estrangement. And she just left the house again—this time, at my request.

Dad walks into the living room. "Are you okay, buddy?" he asks, tentatively.

"I still don't know."

"I'm sorry to spring that on you. When she came here earlier this evening, I was as shocked as you. But we talked. We were discussing when she should meet you and Mona when you arrived. You kind of made the decision for us."

"Did she tell you... What did she tell you?"

"Come on, take a seat." He taps my shoulder. "You look exhausted."

We sit side by side. It's still the same sofa, still the same room from yesterday, but now it seems different, unfamiliar. Like my mother's presence changed everything about it, like her visit changed my reality.

"She's been living abroad," Dad says. "A quiet life. No family. She's a nurse of some kind."

A quiet life. No family. She's a mother with no family. And here we are: a family with no mother. And my Dad has no wife.

"How are *you* holding up?" I ask him.

He shows me a tentative smile. "Not too bad. I've had years to prepare for this moment, but I wasn't expecting it. Not even looking forward to it, to be completely honest. But I knew this day might come. And it did."

"That's a non-answer."

Dad shrugs. "I'm still not sure what she means by showing up. She said she wanted to reconnect with you kids, but we haven't discussed... us, if that's what you're asking. At least Patricia and I are on the same page: this is about you and Mona."

Patricia. It's weird having a name for her. Dad rarely speaks her name; I had almost forgotten it. Now it has a face to match it.

"I need to talk to Mona." He taps my leg and stands up.

I stand up too. "No, let me do that."

"You?" He gives me a doubtful look, his eyebrows arched. In his mind, Mona and I argue and bicker all the time.

"Give me some credit," I reassure him. "She'll listen to me."

"If you're sure... I'll be here if you need me."

"Yeah... I don't think any of us will sleep tonight."

While I walk upstairs, my mind races. Even with all the witch mess, the most pressing issue for Mona and me is our mother's return. We are drained of energy and emotionally spent. Maybe neither of us can deal with the revelation. I feel a little heartless, but I had to send—Patricia? Mom?—away with the promise to contact her later.

I hesitate in front of Mona's door. I'm about to knock when she yells from other side.

"Go away!"

"It's me," I whisper.

"I know. Go away."

I try the knob. It turns, and I open the door.

Mona is slouching, leaning on the headboard and grabbing a pillow as a security blanket. Her expression is contorted as if her face couldn't decide between anger and sadness and settled for a mashup of both.

"Did you talk to her?" she asks.

I sit by the side of her bed. "No, I sent her away. I'll try to meet her tomorrow, though. Wanna come?"

"Not a chance." Her voice is rough, like sandpaper.

"Come on, Mona. Let's hear what she has to say. Aren't you a little curious?"

"Argh!" Mona buries her head into the pillow. "I can't deal with this right now." Her words are muffled. "I messed up with the green light thing. A witch assassin tried to kill me. Skye left. Pain kissed me. It's too much!"

"I know," I say, trying to use a soothing voice. "It's okay if you don't want to go, but we can't ignore her. I'll meet her. And Mona?"

"What?"

"She's a witch too."

She emerges from behind the pillow, looking bewildered. "That's just *great*."

***

Dad spends the night on the sofa, watching Law & Order reruns until he dozes off.

I stay up until three in the morning, when my body finally crumbles under the physical and emotional exhaustion of the previous day. Around sunrise, the garbage truck wakes me up.

My mother calls on my burner phone later in the morning, as I expected.

"Drake? Can you talk?"

"Yes. Do you remember Discovery Park? It has only a few visitors this time of the year. Meet me by the lighthouse at one p.m."

"Okay," she says. I hear her breathe on the phone. "See you soon."

I hang up. I knock on Mona's door, but no one answers. I open the door just a sliver, and see that she is still sleeping. I want to ask if she wants to join me, but she made her position clear last night.

It's still early. I decide to drop by Boulder's house first and see how he's doing.

I grab my jacket and take off in my Volvo. I look in the rearview mirror to see if anyone is following me. I go around the block twice, but nothing seems different. Either Skye was wrong or the witches are much more discreet than I expect.

The drive to Boulder's is uneventful. I park in the same spot I did yesterday and walk to the front door. Before I can ring the bell, the door opens. Boulder's father greets me with a huge smile.

"Come on in," Jeff says.

As soon as he closes the door, he gives me a bear hug and says, "Thank you, Drake, for bringing my boy back."

I don't want it to turn into a sob fest, so I just smile. "Hey, I needed my friend back too. Is he still in the room downstairs?" I point to the door.

Jeff composes himself. "Yes. He's out of the coma, but he still sleeps a lot. The doctors say it's normal. He has trouble speaking, focusing his eyes, and making movements, but it will all come back with time. Well, time and months of physical therapy. They did some tests: the brain swelling is almost completely gone. The chances of a full recovery are good."

The smile he shows me has no bounds.

The door opens, and Serena, the nurse, comes out of the room. When she sees me, her eyes narrow. "You…" I expect a long sermon, but she's brief. "You did good." Her expression is stern, though, and she rubs her golden cross pendant. "You can go in. He just woke up."

"Serena, thanks for keeping this between us," I say.

She nods and opens her mouth as if she's about to say something. But she changes her mind and leaves the living room.

"Come on," Jeff says. "Let's go see him." He leads the way.

Boulder's in bed, still looking weak and emaciated. But his eyes are open. That makes all the difference in the world.

"Son, look who's here. Drake came to visit you."

Boulder's gaze pinballs all over the room until it settles on me. His eyes widen.

"Hey, big guy," I say.

His face spasms, which I take as a sign he's making an attempt to smile. He tries to wave, but his arm flails before dropping back to the bed.

"The control will come back soon, son."

Boulder's eyes follow the sound of Jeff's voice, but they come back to me.

I should be shocked at seeing him helpless and without any coordination. Instead, what I feel is an intense joy, a sense of relief and gratefulness. "Boulder, everybody is really happy that you're back. You scared us, buddy."

He blinks.

"Is he…?" I ask Jeff.

"No, he can't communicate yet. He seems to understand what we say, though. Is that right, son?"

Boulder's eyes move less randomly now. I guess he's okay.

"I thought about bringing a book to read to you, but who am I kidding?" I take out Mona's tablet and access ESPN. "Here's what you missed: the Seahawks are on a three-game winning streak!" I sit down in the chair by the side of the table and reads the results and stats from the latest NFL rounds.

Jeff chuckles and pats me on my shoulder. Boulder is staring at me, and I may be imagining things, because I'm pretty sure his mouth just curved up. Voluntarily.

***

Boulder falls back to sleep. Jeff and I leave the room in silence.

"I can't wait for him to start mumbling and talking. Soon he'll be able to answer yes or no questions by squeezing our hands."

"Jeff, I might not show up that often. I can't explain, but I don't want to attract attention to my participation in this."

He stares at me, as if expecting me to elaborate. But he must realize that's all I'm going to tell him. His face relaxes. "Of course, Drake. Besides, he already has Diana and me smothering him. Sean and Priscilla promised to be here every day after school. They came earlier this morning, actually. They asked about you, but I told them the doctors said we shouldn't overwhelm him with too many visitors now."

"Thanks, Jeff."

"Are you kidding? Thank *you*!" He gives me a one-armed hug. "Anything you need, anytime, just let me know."

When I'm back to my car, I feel lighter. I'm dreading meeting my mother, but at least Boulder seems to be on the right path.

Chapter 4: Skye

I left Seattle's gray skies just to be greeted by London's.

Connor's driver picks us up at Heathrow. He wears a full uniform, black leather gloves, and a hat. "Welcome back, sir," he greets Connor. "Did you have a good flight?"

"Yes, thank you." Connor smiles at him. "How are things?"

"Eerily calm with you abroad, sir."

"We will change that soon," Connor says, sneaking a peek at me.

"Yes, sir. Shall we go to the residence?"

"No. Lady DeWees' manor."

"Of course, sir." He closes the door after us and goes to the driver seat.

"Did you leave your manners in America?" Connor whispers to me. "You know Nigel; you could've said hello."

I turn to Connor. "You must be joking. You're leading me to my ruin. I haven't slept the whole flight, dreading it. And you call me out on my manners? Sorry if being courteous is not at the top of my priority list."

I catch the driver in the rearview mirror, raising his eyebrows.

Connor follows my eyes. "Nigel, my good man. The partition, please?"

"Naturally, sir." The partition immediately starts to lift. He is a

Knowing, but that doesn't mean he needs to know everything.

"I'm sorry you haven't slept, Skye, but we're going straight to Lady DeWees' residence. I called ahead, and the Mothers will be joining us later."

This situation is ridiculous. I'm being kidnapped again. Connor uses a velvety voice and shows courtesy, and he may even care about me, but I'm going against my will nevertheless.

I catch my reflection in the car window. My Allure is fighting the bags under my eyes—and losing. My hair is disheveled; my eyes scream exhaustion. So what? My appearance is the last of my concerns. What will I tell them?

We immediately take the M4, and then the M25.

"Where's this residence?" I ask.

"Waddesdon," Connor answers.

I sigh. I wanted to see more of London, to drive through familiar streets. I've lost count of how many times Mum and I made the route from Heathrow to the city and back. Every new movie meant a new airplane, a new hotel room, a new tutor. But this time the ride means a more radical change in my life. A more *permanent* change.

My eyes feel heavy. I slouch on the seat.

***

I wake up disoriented. I'm still in the car, but someone's holding me. I look up. Connor's eyes meet mine. Of all the things waiting for me, waking up in Connor's arms must be one of the least expected.

"I didn't want to wake you. You were so exhausted," he says.

I straighten, my head leaving its cozy place on his shoulder. "Are we there?"

"Almost." He removes a few strands of hair from my face. "Feeling better?"

"A bit," I say. I'm still confused. Why didn't I try to stop Connor's gesture? I don't know how to react to his change of demeanor. Connor's unjerkification process has me stymied.

How can he expect to be close to me when he's the one responsible for my capture and banishment?

Connor points outside the window. Lady DeWees' large estate rolls into view.

We pass by the ivy-covered walls and arrive at the ten-foot-tall wrought iron gate. A guard leaves his post at the security house and motions to Nigel to open his window.

Connor acts fast and lowers his window first. He addresses the guard, "Connor Wallace and Skye Lexington-Ellis to see Lady DeWees. She's expecting us."

The guard glances at both of us in turn and nods. "Very well, sir."

He goes inside and opens the gate. Nigel takes us to the long driveway. To my right, swans swim in an artificial lake with a fountain. To my left, I see a long stable and a fenced area in the distance. We pass by a seemingly endless parade of classic white marble statues. The lush green lawn is so meticulously trimmed it looks like the ground has been painted green.

Up ahead, we see the large façade of DeWees Manor. The three-story Renaissance chateau reminds me of one of the locations Mum worked at during her latest period piece movie. We go around the circular front garden and stop at the entrance, where a butler awaits us.

The place is imposing and looks like it's been recently restored. The twin staircase towers rise against the gray skies, intimidating and ominous. As if I'm not feeling small enough already.

Nigel opens the car door for us, and the butler leads us to the entrance hall. My True Sight tells me a Sister is already inside.

"Lady DeWees is in a meeting. She'll be with you shortly. She has instructed me to lead you to the red drawing room, where you can wait."

"Is there a restroom?" I ask him.

"Certainly, Miss. The powder room is this way, please."

Connor stutter-steps in the same direction, but I give him a "Seriously?" look, and he lets me go to the restroom alone. "I'll be in the drawing room," he says.

In the large bathroom, I see my reflection once again. The bright light coming from the two golden sconces framing the mirror makes me look ghostly—exactly like I feel. I'm a shell of myself, soon to be stripped of my ties with the only world I've ever known. I let the water pool in the basin and splash some on my face. I reach for the pile of hand towels, and I get the one on top. After my face is dry, I soak another towel and put it on the back of my neck.

I sit on the purple ottoman by the door. The cold compress soothes me a little. I throw my towel into the sink and sneak out of the bathroom.

On my way to the drawing room, I sense two witches nearby. I enter the room. Connor is pacing. Lady DeWees has joined him. She's on the phone. When she sees me, she doesn't smile; she just turns on the speakerphone.

"Goddess help me, you will not question my daughter without me present!" Beneath the rage in the words, I recognize Mum's voice.

"Katherine—"

My mother interrupts her. "It's my baby we're talking about. I'm a London Mother, and I must be there for this. I'm on my way to the airport."

"Mum, your movie! Don't walk away; you said it was the role of a lifetime," I say, approaching the phone table.

"Darling! Don't worry about that. Nothing is more important than you. Are you all right? Are they treating you well?"

Lady DeWees straightens and answers for me. "But of course we are. We're not barbarians."

Connor tries to reason. "Katherine, this is a time-sensitive issue. We need to find the Singularity soon. The Night covens will be making their move as we speak."

"Connor, I like you, but you're the one insisting on doing it by the book. All the Mothers must be present, correct?"

He sighs and looks at Lady DeWees, who has her lips pursed.

"We will wait for you, Katherine," my hostess says. "It's only fair."

"This is a stretch of the meaning of 'fair,'" Mum replies. "Very well. I'm on my way. Skye, darling, hang in there. Do not say anything until I'm with you. Love you."

She hangs up, and the three of us in the room stare at one another. Lady DeWees, a woman of seventy who looks twenty years younger, wears a frown that almost negates her Allure. She just stands there, her arms crossed under the low, frilled neckline of her white silk dress.

"I probably should go home and change," I say.

Lady DeWees is taken aback. "Absolutely not. You're staying here."

"Am I a prisoner?"

"Don't be silly. You're a guest here, of course." She raises her eyebrows. "Just don't leave."

I'm about to protest, but what's the use? Instead, I say, "I need my stuff."

She nods. "Someone can go to the Lexington-Ellis residence and pack you a bag for your stay."

"I'll do it," Connor says.

Confused and exhausted, I decide my body needs rest. "Does anyone have a Sleep potion?" I ask.

Chapter 5: Drake

At half past noon, I park in the almost empty lot. I walk to the lighthouse at a slow pace, trying to calm down. The place is deserted—like Mona and I were by our mother.

I can't bring myself to call her "Mom." She *is* my mother, of course, and no other woman has ever come close to replacing her. Dad doesn't have girlfriends. Or he makes us think so. Anyway, "Mom" should be used for mothers who don't disappear from their kids' lives.

Maybe I'll call her by her given name, Patricia.

As I wait, I deliberately look out over the water. I don't want to see her coming. The freezing wind off the Puget Sound lashes at my face, but I don't care. At last, I feel a presence a few feet away and turn around.

"Hello, Drake," she says. She wears a trench coat that looks way too big for her short frame. Last time I saw her I was a preschooler; she looked impossibly tall to me. Now I tower over her. She carries two big-ass cups of steaming Starbucks coffee.

"Hi. There's a bench over there."

She raises both cups in front of her. "Mocha or Latte?"

I point to the left one, and she hands it to me. Instead of thanking her, I ask, "This is not a potion, is it?"

28

"No." She frowns. "Don't worry."

We start to walk toward the bench. "Strange choice of place," she says, her finger drawing a circle in the air.

"It's an open space. No one can approach us without being seen or your witch alarm going off. And you don't need to worry about the Veil." I take a sip.

She stares at me. "You're a knowing Knowing, aren't you?"

I ignore her compliment. "And I can't be seen with any witches now. If we were in the city, someone might pick up your signature, right?"

We sit on the bench, far apart.

"How are you?" she asks. "Your father told me you're a good student."

"I do okay."

"You've grown up so much. You're tall like Ben."

I want to skip the chat and dive right in, but it turns out talking about meaningless things helps me settle down.

"Mona is about your height," I offer. My voice is becoming steadier.

"Yes. She's gorgeous, isn't she?"

That's my cue. "It's her Allure. She wasn't like that."

My mother—Patricia—nods. "Drake, I'm glad that you decided to hear me out. I know I have no right to show up like this. You have all the reason in the world to resent me. Thank you for not throwing it in my face."

"The day is long," I say. Easy, Drake. Hear her side of the story before making judgments.

My jab hits its spot. "I know. I deserve that, and all that you and Mona will say to me."

And Dad, I think, but I keep my mouth shut.

She continues. "I won't ask you to believe me right away. You probably won't agree with my decision and my motives. If it were a few years ago, I could get away with 'You'll understand when you grow up,' but you're already grown up. Now you can understand, but you also might think differently."

"Okay, enough with the disclaimer. I've waited years for the reasons, but I don't think I can wait much longer." I set my cup of coffee on the concrete underneath the bench.

She lowers her head and takes a deep breath. "Over the years, I rehearsed this talk many times. I hope I can... convey how hard those decisions were for me. I didn't make them lightly; I knew there would be terrible consequences for all of us." She raises her head. "I'm a witch, Drake. I was a Night Sister. And a witch assassin."

"An assassin?" All the outside cold seems to have reached my blood, my chest.

"'Was.' That's why I had to leave you."

I'm too stunned to talk. It turns out this stranger in front of me is much stranger than I ever thought.

"I come from a family of Night Sisters. Even before my Daybreak, I'd been trained to be one. When they found out about my... potential, they pegged me as a future witch assassin."

"Like the Scythe woman?"

"Yes. Scythe is one of the reasons I'm here. She's as good as I was. I mean, as *skilled* as I was."

"Did you murder anyone?" I ask.

"I was an assassin, Drake," she says softly. "They called me 'Fury.'"

I put my hands on my head. "I didn't expect this to get worse, but you've managed it."

"Hear me out. I did it for three years, but I wasn't cut out for it. I don't think anybody is, really. I changed my mind quickly, but it's hard to disentangle yourself from that world. I only lasted three years because I was plotting my getaway. I had to get money, forge a new identity, and hatch an escape plan."

"And it took you three years?"

"It's more complicated than you think. In my second year on the job, my parents were killed in a coven war, and my coven—my Night coven—was a paranoid one. But finally I was able to fake my death and escape to the U.S."

I'm glad that Mona didn't come. It would be too much for her. "Wait, my grandparents were murdered? And you're not American?"

"No, Drake. You're part Italian. I had to work hard to lose the accent. And you knew my parents were deceased. You now know the why and the how."

"Wait. What's your real name?"

"It doesn't matter. I haven't used it for twenty years now."

"Humor me."

She stares at me. "Beatrice Caprese," she says in a rush of words. "Oh, Goddess, I thought I'd never utter that name again."

I stand up and pace the patch of grass in front of the bench. "You're just a nesting doll of fake identities and lies, aren't you?"

"Please let me finish. I came to Seattle and started to study nursing. I met your father. We dated, and we married. You were born a year later."

I scoff.

"What?"

"You didn't say, 'I fell in love with your father.'"

She raises her chin. "I didn't. I liked him as much as I've ever liked anybody. He's a good man—a great man. And he gave me you and Mona."

"And yet, you gave up on us!"

"We will get to that. But you need to understand. Someone with my past doesn't fall in love. It doesn't work that way. We... I was too closed—still am. I never let my defenses down enough to love someone, to have some fairy tale marriage. I cared deeply for him. And I love my kids unconditionally."

I sit down again, grab my forgotten cup, and take a sip. It's not warm anymore. "Go on."

"I was settled. I was happy—we all were. I had achieved a level of joy that was unthinkable to me a few years before. And then I learned the Night covens had found out about my fake death. They were after me."

"Why?"

"They're deeply revengeful. Also, I'm a walking record of many of their crimes. They wanted to cover their tracks." She takes a deep breath. Her coffee is untouched. "I had to make a choice—a terrible choice. For two weeks, I was on the edge. And then news reached me that they were getting closer. On that day, the decision became easy. I had to leave you all in order to protect you."

It's as if I'm being pierced by a thousand daggers. I feel sick.

"Do you understand, Drake? They wouldn't spare you—none of you. That's their way. My only choice was to flee and draw their attention to me. I left a trail leading them after me in Europe. I spent five months being a step ahead of them, and then I fled to Rwanda. I adopted a new identity and used my nursing degree to get a job, first with the Red Cross, then with other associations. I've been there since, laying low and staying out of big cities for fear of being recognized. I sometimes use my magic to help the ailing patients. Every time I sensed a Sister nearby, I would go away—covens are not part of my life anymore. But I kept an eye on you all this time. I have a Sister friend, someone I trust, who makes the inquiries for me."

"So, you were Beatrice. You were Fury. You were Patricia Hunter, and Patricia Burke before getting married. And now your name is?"

She casts her eyes down. "My current identity is Jennifer Sullivan."

"And yet… you're none of these people. Who are you?"

"I *am* Jennifer Sullivan. I'm not the witch assassin, not the mother who abandoned you. But I'm the one who has been trying to atone for all my past mistakes. I've been Jennifer for thirteen years. Thirteen! Jennifer's life is worthy. I try to do good deeds and help others. It'll never erase what I did, but it may compensate for it somehow. I am Jennifer."

She finally looks at me. "I have to believe I'm her. Because if I'm any of the others, I'm a monster."

Chapter 6: Skye

My thoughts bounce around my head like a pinball. Even the concept of time is blurry to me. Yesterday afternoon I was in Seattle, doing a great job of fooling Connor and Vanessa, his assistant. The Dispel potion had countered the Truth potion they injected in me. They were willing to accept anything I said. I was almost scot-free.

Then Mona lost control of her magic again, and the burst of green light energy sealed all of our fates.

I left Seattle the same night. The flight took ten hours, and London is eight hours ahead. My internal clock is completely messed up; I'm exhausted, and I still can't sleep. I decide to try anyway. Maybe I just need to lie down and let the night pass me by.

But before I can go to the bedroom that Lady DeWees assigned to me, Judi comes to visit me.

She's Mum's best friend, but she's more than that: Judi is the Sister who taught me so much and who I love like family. I rush to her and give a warm and overdue hug.

"Skye, how are you?"

I take her hands in mine. "I've arrived few hours ago. I was about to get some sleep, but that can wait. I'm so happy to see you."

Judi smiles at me. Her white hair is tied in a bun. She wears a long coat over her dark green dress. "I'm glad too. We have so much to talk about!"

The butler shows up out of nowhere to collect her coat just as she's getting out of it.

I take her by the arm and lead her to the now empty library. I saw Connor going to the dining room earlier. The energy I feel emanating from upstairs is Lady DeWees'. She must have gone to bed. Lucky witch.

Judi and I sit on the large sofa. She runs her hands through my hair. "You look tired."

"I had a long day. It started in Seattle twenty hours ago. I couldn't sleep on the plane."

She nods. "I can imagine. How are things? Did you tell them anything?"

I like how she uses the word "them." As if it is them against us. She's on my side, and that's important to hear.

"No," I say. "It wouldn't matter, because they wouldn't believe me anyway. They need Elsa Dunivant here to make sure I'm telling the truth once and for all."

"I'm surprised Elsa hasn't been summoned already." She looks around as if she expects Elsa to pop out of a corner of the room.

"Well, Mum called and raised hell. She doesn't want them interrogating me without her present."

Judi smirks and taps my hand. "This sounds like Katherine, all right."

"Thanks for being here for me."

She leans back. "But of course, Skye. You're not my daughter, but you are my little girl."

I look down at the rich carpet. "Aren't you ashamed of me?"

Judi puts her finger under my chin and lifts my head gently.

"Never. I know you. I know there's a very good reason for what you did. You wouldn't do it lightly."

A smile reaches my lips. "Please be my defense witness and tell them exactly that."

She chuckles. "I will. And I can do much more than that. Now, who do I have to kill to get a decent cup of tea in this house?"

***

Judi stays for about an hour, telling me the latest coven news. The Mothers are appalled at the green light energy outburst.

"That's an understatement. There has never been a more blatant attempt to break the Veil," an angry voice says from the library's door. Lady DeWees is there in a frilly white nightgown.

I had sensed her coming, so I'm not surprised, but Judi raises her eyebrows.

"Hello, Camilla," Judi says in a sweet voice. "I hope we haven't been talking too loud."

Judi's politeness disarms Lady DeWees. "Oh, not at all. I sensed another signature at the house, and I needed to know who was visiting."

"Sorry to wake you up," Judi continues in her charm offensive. She's sweet, but also smart. She knows that she can soften Lady DeWees.

"But it's no trouble at all! I volunteered to host Skye. If it gives me a chance to see my Sisters, that's all for the better." Lady DeWees even smiles at Judi!

But then she looks at me with disapproving eyes.

"I'm in deep trouble, aren't I?" I ask.

Lady DeWees paces the room. "I know you don't like me, but you need to understand. This is serious, Skye. This whole thing

36

threatens our way of life. This is exactly what we feared from the beginning. Leaving the Singularity unchecked can cause all sorts of trouble for us, some of it disastrous. I can't fathom why you did what you did, but you need to understand that."

"I *did* have a handle on it," I say, frustrated. "Things got out of control."

"Goddess, Skye!" She slaps the coffee table, making the delicate porcelain cups and silver spoons clink against one another. All the goodwill that Judi built is gone now. "There was an earthquake. A school fire. Can you imagine if children had gotten hurt? And now this green light all over the internet. How many signs do you need?" Her voice goes down. "This was never under control."

Her scolding is not unfair. I can see her point. But the fire and the earthquake happened before I knew it was Mona. And the green light happened because I trusted her and Drake. I know I'm at fault, but it's not as simple as Lady DeWees thinks. I wish I could tell her.

But even when I tell her, she won't believe my good intentions.

Lady DeWees is not finished. "And that poor girl in the hospital… Who is she, Skye? A conveniently hurt girl you decided to blame? Now we have to wake her up even if it kills her. If you don't talk, we will summon a small army of Healing Touch Sisters to wake her up and learn the Singularity's true identity." Her eyes pierce me. "You know we have no option, right?"

I sustain her stare, but inside I'm terrified. I won't let anything happen to Brianna. I'm going to delay my inevitable confession, but I'll tell them before Brianna is harmed.

"That's not what the true Craft is about," I say.

My host isn't swayed. "If we have to choose between the Veil and the Singularity, we protect the Veil. We have magic, but we live in the real world, Skye."

The three of us stay silent, pondering that implication.

Eventually, Judi says, "Well, it's late. It seems my work here is done. Camilla, thanks for spearheading this. Skye, please have a good night's rest. You are going to need it."

Chapter 7: Drake

I've always half-jokingly imagined that my mother was a super-spy. And I ended being right. Only she's not James Bond, she's a James Bond *villain*.

From time to time, she stares at me. It doesn't bother me. She hasn't seen me in thirteen years.

"Why are you here?" We need to rip off this Band-aid soon.

"Mona, of course. The Singularity."

Her conviction is so strong I don't deny it. "When did you figure it out? When she was a baby?"

She lets out a bitter chuckle. "I didn't even know she was a witch. Little kids who are Sisters have the faintest magical signature, but neither Mona nor you released anything. I was relieved that neither of you kids was a witch. I have known only sorrow because I'm one."

That stings me a bit. I never thought about having magical powers. But it would be nice to have *something* special. "How, then?"

"A Sister told me about the Singularity's arrival. She's my only Sister friend, and I don't talk to her often. She visits me every few weeks. According to her, the big release of energy two years ago was on everyone's mind. Every Sister in the world heard about it. But I didn't pay attention. I mean, I'm not even privy to coven talk anymore. I knew it had happened on the West Coast of the US, but that's a vast region. Mona was only thirteen at the time, and I didn't know she was a witch to begin with. I never made the connection."

She sighs. "But when the earthquake hit Seattle, I started to get suspicious. Mona didn't release energy as a baby, but the rumors were that the Singularity's energy worked differently. Mona was at Daybreak age then—it was very close to her birthday. And it had happened in Seattle. Even if Mona wasn't the Singularity, she was too close to the event. My friend told me the girl they identified—"

"Brianna," I offer.

"Yes. That she was living in the same area I used to live in. I had to see for myself."

It's too much to absorb in one sitting. I stand up and pace. The grass is sleeping for the winter, and it looks dead. I kick a patch. "You followed us that day in the car. When Skye snapped your picture."

She nods. "Yes. I saw your girlfriend in the park."

"And at Mona's dance?"

She looks down. "It was my little girl's dance. I needed to see her. I know I may not deserve it, but I had to be there. And, once again, your girlfriend noticed I was there. How does she do it?"

I straighten. "Beats me," I say.

Patricia's features harden for a second. "Come on, Drake. I'm very good at hiding; I've been trained since I was a kid and stayed out of sight for over a decade. How does she—"

"Skye. Her name's Skye." My voice hardens without me noticing.

"How does Skye know where I am at all times?"

My active imagination takes over. What if she is still a Night witch, trying to gain my trust? Even if she's not part of the Night covens anymore, she still could be a renegade, like Jane—maybe she

40

would like Mona's powers for herself. I shudder thinking of a confessed witch assassin with all that magic.

You're too trustworthy, Drake. That's what Skye told me once. I trust everyone, see the best in everyone. Not only that, I *expect* the best in everyone. Right now, I'm already gambling by letting Jane into our lives. I should protect myself and my family better. Be more guarded, be less eager to believe everybody.

Even as I make the argument in my head, I know it's pointless. I am who I am. I trust people. If my long lost mother wants to backstab me, what's the point, anyway?

I have to trust her. Besides, I don't know if Charms are a big secret among the witches. "She has True Sight Charm."

Patricia leans back on the bench. "Really? Wow. That's pretty rare."

"I've been told."

"It would have been very useful in my old line of work. Just saying." She grins.

She has a bit of my sense of humor. I'm not sure how this makes me feel.

"I can imagine," I reply.

"You sure know how to pick them."

I just nod, hoping my face is expressionless.

"Tell me about your girlfriend."

"Well, to begin with we should probably use the 'ex' prefix from now on."

"Oh," she says. "You okay?"

I'm not ready to buddy up to her yet. I kick another patch of grass. "Yeah. She's from London, and she's the one who found out about Mona. We both did, actually. But, to protect Mona, she decided to tell everyone that the girl in a coma, Brianna, was the Singularity."

"But… Are you okay?"

"Let's not do that right now."

"Okay." She lowers her voice. "What are your thoughts?"

Where to begin? I hesitate and shake my head. I've had so many thoughts over the years. So many theories. Maybe that's it. I'll share one of my theories.

"Do you realize… Mona and I thought all these years that you leaving was all our fault! Dad never said it, but I bet he thought *he* was the reason. Mothers don't abandon their kids."

She flinches as if I had threatened to hit her. "I know. But not all mothers are the same, not all the situations are the same. Mothers usually are not witch assassins that put their families at risk. I know many wouldn't have made the decision I made. But that's the thing: it was *my* decision to make. I can't make my decision based on what other people would have done."

"You're an assassin. Help us fight for Mona."

"No, I can't fight. I vowed not to do it again. Even if I wanted to, I haven't trained for fifteen years. I'm the opposite of what I once was. I'm a healer now."

I run my fingers through my hair. "You've got to help Mona!"

"I want to, more than anything. But if I stay too close, they will sense me. I could put you in danger."

"That ship has sailed. We're all already in danger. The Night covens are after us. They couldn't care less about you. They want the big prize. Mona. She's still your daughter, you know. She's still your responsibility."

This finally breaks through her wall of togetherness. Her eyes water. "You're right. You both will always be my responsibility." She wipes away a few tears and looks at the Sound.

My gaze also turns to the water. I let her have those few moments.

***

We walk back to our cars. I'm surprised that Discovery Park is almost empty; in Seattle, even sub-zero temperatures and icy wind can't discourage joggers and hikers. The park's large open spaces feel devoid of life. At least I'm sure neither of us was followed.

"I need to tell you something," she blurts out. "I have the Persuasion Charm. Do you know what that is?"

"I can guess, based on the name." Patricia has Persuasion, then. I wonder if she's manipulating me.

She sees my face and hurries to add, "You need to know that I wasn't counting on that during our talk. You know I can't turn it off, but everything I told you, then and now, is the truth. Anyway, you should know. I don't want to influence you."

"I believe you," I tell her.

Only two cars occupy the enormous lot: my old Volvo and her silver Focus, parked right next to each other.

"You have my number," she says.

"And you can call me on this phone. Don't come to our house. If you need to talk to Dad, please arrange a meeting somewhere else." Then I realize we haven't discussed this part yet. "You *are* talking to Dad, right?"

Her eyes shift a little. "We talked last night. I haven't told him anything about the Sister stuff yet."

I shove my hands in my pockets. "Do you think it's going to be necessary? Telling him about Mona, I mean?"

"If the covens figure it out, I may need to run away with her. Ben should know about it, maybe before it happens."

"Wait… You want to run away with her?" The air I suck into my lungs suddenly feels freezing cold.

"We'd need to hide her. And protect her. I know how to do both."

"I doubt she would agree to that."

"Would you?"

"I haven't thought about it."

"Well, think about it. And if you agree with me, convince her. I'm her best shot."

I say nothing.

Patricia mistakes my silence as a dismissal. "Okay, then. See you later. Right?"

She's making an awesome effort of giving me my space and not assuming anything. I like that. She gets it. My mixed feelings tip one way, and I step forward and give her a hug that's unexpected, even for me. She hugs me back, tight, and then she lets me go.

"Right." I enter my car, turn the key, crank the heat to the max, and drive away.

***

I don't want to go home. If I do, Mona and Dad will ask me about the meeting, if not directly, at least with their eyes. Since my poor mind hasn't processed it yet, I wouldn't know what to tell them.

It's not as simple as being happy or angry with her return. Those are not the only options; they aren't even mutually exclusive. Figuring out what it means is too much for me now.

Sean must be at Boulder's, and I can't go back there—Boulder needs quiet for now. If I visit Pri, she'll bombard me with questions

44

about Skye. Pri left a few messages for me this morning, but I'm ignoring her for now.

Since I have my backpack, I decide to go for a swim. Like I would if this were just another day. Nothing suspicious there, right? If the witches are following me, I'd better stick to my routine. Swimming is my meditation technique. I need to clear my mind and figure out my next steps.

I change and go to the pool deck. No one's here this Sunday. I stretch and do a few lazy laps to warm up. Coach Summers told me to improve my backstroke; I'm drifting to the left for some reason and need to keep correcting my course.

The empty pool building is silent but for the sounds of my arms hitting the water. My steady swimming, the loneliness, the stillness around me, and the water encasing my body make it feel like I'm in an isolation chamber.

I'm focused on my mechanics when I notice someone enter the pool building. It breaks the illusion of having my own world. I stop and remove my goggles.

Yara is at the edge of the pool, smiling at me. "I knew I'd find you here."

"Hey, Yara." I look at the building entrance.

"No one else is here. We're safe." She crouches down and motions for me to get closer.

I dive beneath the lane separators until I'm holding onto the edge of the pool, at her feet.

"You okay?" she asks.

"Yeah. A little stiff." Scythe, the witch assassin, shot me with a Paralysis potion yesterday when we helped Boulder. "Thanks again for dragging me away from danger."

"From danger," she repeats, adding a fake eerie tone to her voice. She giggles at her own joke. "Sure." She dips her hand in the water. "It's not that cold. Mind if I join you?"

"Er... no."

She chuckles. "Okay."

I go back to my slow strokes. I haven't swum half a length of the pool when I hear her splash. Wow, is Yara back from the locker room already? I look behind me. She's gliding under the water, coming in my direction. When she emerges, inches from me, her face glistens with a thin layer of water. She shakes her curly black hair, splashing droplets on me.

"This is good. No wonder you love it," she says.

My eyes flicker to her body. "Uh, Yara, are you naked?"

She laughs. "You wish. No, silly, this is my skin-colored underwear. See?" She points to an almost invisible caramel bra strap on her shoulder.

"I can hardly see it. Wait. You planned this, didn't you?"

She shakes her head, once again sending drops of water on me. "No! Give me some credit, Drake. I can be much more forward than that. Come on! Race you." She dives and emerges in the lane next to mine.

"Race me?" I repeat.

"Readysetgo!" She takes off.

I go after her. It's automatic for me. I'm way taller than her, so I give maybe fifty percent. After three strokes, I peek behind me. She's not there. She's ahead of me! I decide to take it seriously and catch up to her, but we tap the end almost at the same time.

"First!" she yells immediately.

"No way. I beat you."

"Again?"

"Readysetgo!" I say.

But I slow down so she can keep up with me. Her strokes are perfect, economic. Her legs kick with the exact range. It's like she's flying underwater. I keep breathing to my right to catch glimpses of her.

We race neck and neck until we tap simultaneously again.

"Beat ya!" she says.

"I'll give that one to you. Your form is perfect!"

"Thank you. You're hot too."

"I mean your *swimming* form."

She chuckles. "Right. I saw you checking me out."

In spite of myself, I smirk. "Where did you learn how to swim like that?"

She shows me the silver mermaid tat on her arm. "Oh, I have a little bit of mermaid blood."

"What?" My breath gets even shallower.

"Just kidding! I learned it very young. But enough about me." She comes to my lane and puts her hands on the edge of the pool behind me, trapping me. "I've heard you're single now." Her gaze flickers from my eyes to my mouth and back.

"Yara…"

Her dark brown eyes are locked on mine. "No one will ever know," she whispers. Her warm breath is enticing.

"I would," I say firmly.

She smirks and floats away, releasing me from my makeshift prison. But she's not mad. "You really love her! That's so cool."

Her smile confuses me. "Aren't you upset?"

She splashes water on my face. "No. You know I could've just brewed a powerful Fancy Me potion and keep you on a leash for as long as I wanted, right? But I'd never do that. It's not you that I want. I want what you have with her. The real thing."

I finally get what she means. "You will. I mean, you'll have it even better than me. Skye and I are not together anymore. But why have you been flirting with me?"

She back floats in the water. Her almost invisible underwear tries to get my attention again. "At first I thought you were a player. I thought I had a chance with you. Until you told me you loved her. Remember? When you asked me to help Mona? I had Truth potion laced through my cigarette smoke, did you know?"

"Yara!" I want to be mad at her, but I'm intrigued by her ingenuity.

"And now Skye is away. She left you, even though you did the right thing for Boulder. You could have had me, just now. But you *still* love her."

"I do." Treading water becomes a little harder for me, as if the weight of my worrying is dragging me down. "I'm sorry for this situation. Are we okay?"

"Of course. Now, how are we getting her back for you?"

"'We'? You want to help me?"

Yara returns to an upright position, faces me, and winks. "I'm a sucker for love stories."

"This one might not have a happy ending. She's in London, about to out Mona and be banished from her coven. Oh, yeah, and she hates me."

"Don't worry. I know a few tricks." She swims to the pool ladder. "Now look away while I dress myself. Fun time is over, D. Time to get your lady back."

48

Chapter 8: Skye

I wake up in a strange, dark room and wait for my eyes to adjust. The moonlight allows me to see. The softness of the mattress almost lulls me back to sleep, but soon I recall who I am and what I'm facing. I look up, as if asking the Goddess for answers. I doubt that she'll give me any, but I feel an overwhelming desire to pray.

The four poster bed I lay in has a large headboard carved with triquetras. Long crimson drapes hang from the top. It's supposed to make the bed cozy, but to me it feels like a cage. I shudder and climb out of bed.

Even with the radiators on, the night feels cold. I can sense two sources of magical energy in the house. One is Lady DeWees, of course, but I can only guess about the other.

Still in my pajamas, I open the door to my room. No one in the hallway. I walk down the stairs. The moonlight coming through the large windows guides me.

On the ground floor, the guard is sitting in an armchair.

He looks up from his book. "May I help you?" He's not rude, but he's not friendly either.

"I want to walk outside."

He doesn't blink an eye; he must be used to our witch ways. He nods in the direction of a garden room at the back of the manor.

If he's not concerned with me running away, then they must have a guard outside, too.

My steps echo on the vestibule's wooden floor. I open the French doors to the terrace and see the full moon lurking behind the clouds. A flower garden behind the gazebo seems to beckon. I walk there with confidence. I kneel in the gazebo's garden, my fingers digging into the soil that feeds the daphne and witch hazel beneath me. I don't have my candles and oils; it's just the earth and me. I ask the Goddess for strength and forgiveness. My personal magic flows inside me, making me alive, alert, and confident. My prayer is a whisper, and the response is silent. No words, no epiphanies, only serenity.

The Goddess knows. Maybe that's all I need.

I still have no answers, but now I'm ready.

***

When I return from my reinvigorating ritual, my body tingles with True Sight. The buzzing sensation tells me a source of magical energy is coming in my direction from inside the house. Someone saw me in the garden or was warned by the guard.

Connor meets me by the stairs. He's wearing a tight v-neck shirt and cotton pajama pants. "Out for a walk?" he asks casually.

"I couldn't sleep," I say.

"I can't blame you. How are you feeling?"

"Awake."

"Yeah. The jetlag is killing me too. Let's get a cup of tea." Without waiting for my response, he leads me into the kitchen.

I sit by the ancient wood table while he turns on the stove top and fills a teakettle.

While the water heats, he joins me. He sits down and puts his hand over mine.

"Connor…"

"Just hear me out. Please?"

I nod. Our hands still touch.

"I realize now it's not the best of times to bring this up, but have you given any thought to our talk a while ago?"

He doesn't specify, but I know what he means: if I'd consider getting back together.

My silence forces him to go on. "Please don't think I'm pressuring you for an answer. I know this is bad timing. I just would like to know if there's even a tiny chance, now that you're—"

"'Free'? I don't feel free."

"I was about to say 'not committed.'" His eyes hold my stare.

His warm hand touching mine brings back memories, some good, some bad. We were together. Since we dated, he's been all muscles and raw strength, always a man even when other guys his age were boys. It's hard not to be fascinated by him, not wanting to be with him. But Connor's Trust Charm sometimes works against him: I know about it, and I have always wondered if my feelings were true or a result of his magic.

He leans over, his eyes never leaving mine. When he kisses me, I let him. I close my eyes. I even kiss him back.

But my body doesn't respond. I was looking for human contact, any contact, but I don't feel the spark. Actually, I feel the opposite, as if I'm indifferent to it.

The teakettle whistles, jolting us out of our kiss. We look at each other, but neither of us smiles. The whistle becomes louder until Connor breaks eye contact and goes to attend to it.

For the first time ever, I have a physical longing for someone. I miss Drake. I miss his body, his embrace, his smell. And his touch, most of all.

While Connor pours the water into two porcelain cups with teabags, it dawns on me.

That's my answer. It's not any human contact I miss; it's Drake's.

"Connor, I have your answer."

He nods, his face hardening. Maybe he already knows what's coming.

"I want to be honest, but I don't want to hurt your feelings," I whisper.

"Skye, I'm a strong guy. I can take it." He smiles with his lips only; his eyes don't follow suit.

I motion for him to sit down, and now it's my turn to take his hand in mine.

"Connor, I wasn't cold or distant or withdrawn. I simply didn't love you."

He winces. "Maybe I overestimated my strength."

"I didn't mean it that way. What I'm saying is that we were never supposed to be together. We like each other. I admire you."

"But you've never loved me."

"How could I? I was in love with the *idea* of you. You were two years older, the coven's golden-boy, smart, and you look like... you. Any sixteen-year-old girl would be head over heels."

He scoffs, but he doesn't withdraw his hand. "What about me, Skye? Have you ever thought that maybe I loved you?"

"But you didn't! That's what struck me now. You were also infatuated with what I could have become. Your little queen. You thought you could mold me into a female version of you. We would be the perfect couple. But I was too young. Not only that, but I wasn't that person. I will never be. And when you realized it, you treated me... like you did."

His shoulders hunch. He looks away from me, his stare vacant. But he still grips my hand. "I'm sorry. For everything." His voice doesn't crack, but it's softer.

I put my hand on his chin and turn his head, forcing him to face me. "I'm sorry too, Connor. Can you see? We're not meant to be."

He nods and gives me a tiny, forced smile. Then his spine becomes straight, and he says, "I need to tell you something."

"Okay..."

He takes his time. "Wow, this is hard."

"Just say it."

He looks at me with sad eyes and blurts out. "I know I can never make up for all the pain that I caused you, but I hope you can someday forgive me."

I never expected this apology. It's only now that it is offered that I realize that I wanted it. That I needed it to move on.

"Of course. It's done. It's in the past." I suppress a tear.

He grips my hand with even more strength now, and I do the same. I don't want to let go. We will never belong to each other, but I don't want him out of my life.

We stay like that for a long time while our tea gets cold.

Chapter 9: Drake

Mona said to act normal. She told me that if we went to school and did everything like we always do, the covens, good ones and bad ones, wouldn't have a reason to suspect us.

How weird is that I'm following my little sister's advice?

School this Monday feels anything but typical. It was bad enough after Boulder's accident. We only noticed he was a big part of our lives—with his attitude, his swagger, his infamous Boulderisms—after he wasn't present anymore.

And, for me, Skye's absence is many times more unsettling.

Sean spots me parking the car and comes over.

"Hey, D-Man." We do our bro handshake.

"Hey, Sean. I saw Boulder yesterday." I get my backpack and lock the car. We walk to the school building.

He nods. "Me too. Arrived just after you left. He looks bad, but he looks good, right?"

Leave it to Sean to summarize the situation accurately in the simplest terms possible.

"You nailed it. Talking like a real writer, my man," I tell him. "How's the movie business?"

Sean shrugs. "The screenplay is coming along."

It's weird seeing him so focused and low-key. It's not the Boulder thing; he really changed.

"Let's talk to the Weird Sisters," he says, pointing to Greta and Yara. Well, at least some of the old Sean remains.

"Hey, guys," Greta says. "Good news about Boulder, huh? Do you think it's okay if I visit?"

"Sure, why not?" Sean says.

She bites her lip. "Do you think Pri would be okay with it?"

"Come on," I tell her. "He's your friend. You don't need permission, and you don't need to worry." Petty jealousy is at least part of the reason why Boulder was in a coma. I need to believe that none of us will let that happen again.

"Okay. Did you guys see that green light on Saturday? Crazy crap, right?" Greta says that staring at me.

"Yeah?" I say. I look at Yara, who is looking at the throng of students like she isn't interested in the conversation. I guess she didn't tell Greta.

"Yeah," Greta goes on. "Everybody's talking about it."

No kidding. Most of the kids in Fremont High must have seen the green light and heard the clinking sounds. But only Greta recognized it for what it was: a big mess of magical energy. And she knows I'm a Knowing. Since Skye is not here and Yara apparently didn't talk, I'm the only one left to ask.

I say nothing. Sean tells Greta about Boulder's recovery while the four of us cross the parking lot. Yara and I hang back a little.

"If you want to plot to get Skye back, drop by my house after school one of these days," she whispers to me.

Now that Yara and I have agreed to kill any possibility of romance between us, I feel more comfortable around her. And at ease with her invitation. "I will," I say.

Priscilla is sitting by herself on the front steps of the school. She springs to her feet when she sees me.

"I'll catch up with you," I tell Sean and the girls. "Hey, Pri. What's up?"

Her eyes move sideways, telling me to go to a more private place. We walk to a tree, away from the other students. "Did you hear from Skye?"

"No. She's still not returning your calls?"

Pri pouts, looking dejected. "I called her cell, and her home number in London. No answer. I called her house here too, but Gemma said she had an emergency. She didn't have any other number to try."

"I'm in the same boat. She isn't talking to me. She must have had a good reason to bolt so suddenly. I think it's her mother's health again." I hate lying to Pri, but what's the alternative?

She shakes her head. "It sounds fishy. Of course Gemma would know how to reach her if she needed to. And the other time she vanished from school, she talked to me. But this time, nothing. Why aren't you worried? Is she your girlfriend or what?"

I scratch my head. "I think she's 'or what' now…"

Pri takes a step toward me. "What do you mean?"

"We kind of broke up."

"What? Again?" She crosses her arms. "Why?"

I avert her eyes. "It's complicated. I'm not even sure."

The bell rings, but neither of us moves.

Pri's voice becomes harsh. "I love that girl, but she tests my patience sometimes. Why aren't you pissed? It's the second time she's done this to you."

"I guess she had her reasons."

56

Pri uncrosses her arms and puts a hand on my shoulder. "Drake. Get to the bottom of this. Remember when she left the school for a week and you found her holed up at my house? I still don't know exactly what happened."

Skye had been assaulted by the Night covens that time. She was completely bruised and bloody, but she asked for Pri's help. I can only imagine the story that Skye must have told Priscilla then.

Priscilla says, "She never tells us her stuff. Don't you think that's weird? Having so many secrets from her best friend and her boyfriend?"

I shrug.

Her eyes narrow. She knows I'm lying. "I know you! You wouldn't take this quietly like that. You're hiding something too. What's going on?" The hand on my shoulder pushes me back, as if she's trying to jolt the truth out of me.

"Trust me, Priscilla. I wish I knew where this is going." At least, this is partially true.

She takes a deep breath. "I thought Skye and I had a real breakthrough when Boulder was in the hospital. We both came clean about everything. And now this. I'm having friendship whiplash."

I know exactly how she feels.

We exchange glances. She wraps her arm around mine, and we march together into the school building.

***

When school ends, I don't go home. I cross the street to the pool building for swim practice. I promised Coach Summers to join the team and take it seriously.

At first it sounded hard, but it turns out that not having a girlfriend really opens up your schedule.

I still prefer having Skye, though.

The thought makes my shoulders slump. Seattle is particularly gray this afternoon, and the drizzle soaks my gym bag and me. Oh well. I'm about to get wet anyway.

I stretch and do my laps. My times suck, though. Coach Summers is yelling at me, partly to encourage me and partly out of frustration. I don't know what to say. My heart is not in it today.

Once again I linger at the pool after the drill ends. I'm not friends with my teammates, and I don't want to talk to Coach. When I enter the locker room, it's almost empty and the burner phone in my bag is ringing.

I get it and answer it outside the locker area. "Yes?"

"Drake, are you free to meet?" Jane's voice is rushed and commanding, as usual.

"S-sure," I say. My teeth are chattering. I didn't have time to get a towel, and the building door lets in a cold draft.

"Meet me at the Lenin statue in an hour." She hangs up.

I stare at the phone, but soon the freezing air gets the best of me, and I rush back into the locker room for a hot shower.

***

For some reason, Seattle has a statue of Lenin on a street corner. Of course it's in crazy-fun Fremont, the neighborhood that calls itself "The Center of the Universe." The Fremont folks are way quirky and artistic, sometimes beyond my comprehension. A few blocks away from the Lenin statue, there's the Fremont Rocket and the Fremont Troll that I never got the chance to show to Skye.

Today Lenin is wearing a Seahawks jersey. Of course he is.

I stand by the statue, looking for Jane. I see her waving at me from inside a gelato shop. I walk there.

58

"Hey, Jane."

"Hey. Get something. I've been here for an hour, and I already ate two cones."

Apparently, we're not doing how-are-yous today. I go to the counter, get a vanilla cone, and sit with Jane at the window table.

The other patrons steal glances at her, and it's not because of her attitude. She doesn't hide her burned face, and people are curious.

"I never pictured you as having an ice cream with a guy," I say, grinning.

Jane doesn't smile. She points to a building across the street. "I used to live there."

Right. When we were looking for Jane—at the time she was in full psycho mode—Connor told us about Jane's apartment in Fremont. She abandoned it when she ran away from the Night coven that was blackmailing her.

"Do you need to retrieve something from inside?"

"No. I think the Night Sisters may come over to check it. See if they can catch me, or find some clue. If they show up, I'll follow them. Maybe they'll lead me to where Jason is hidden."

Jane and I couldn't be more different, but at least one thing unites us: the Night covens are after our siblings. That counts for something. I understand what she's going through and to what lengths I would go to protect my little sister.

"Do you need my help? I can go there. They don't know me."

"No, it's too risky."

"Come on, I'm here already. That's why you asked me to come, right?"

She looks past me, but not at the building. "No. I just wanted to ask you if Skye's coming back. With her here, we could find Jason much faster."

"Yeah… The witch radar thing." I bite into my cone. "The thing is… I'm not sure what she's doing. You should probably plan this thing without her."

"Where *is* Skye? I thought she'd take part in this. Does she still hate me?"

I grit my teeth. "Skye left."

"I know she left Seattle."

"Seattle, me, her coven. She dumped me. She's in London, and she'll probably be banished."

To Jane's credit, she doesn't gloat or smirk. On the other hand, she doesn't seem too sorry. Not for me, nor Skye.

Then she gazes away. For someone who's staking a place out, she seems awfully distracted.

"Why did you ask me here, Jane? You could've asked about Skye on the phone."

She looks at me. "You know what? Let's do this. Go to my apartment, see if someone suspicious is there. Here are my keys." She hands me a skull keychain. "The large one is for the building's door; the other one is for my apartment. The number is forty-one."

"Okay… What do I do?"

"Take a look around." She couldn't be vaguer.

I can't shake the feeling that she agreed to my suggestion just to change the subject. But why? I do a mental shrug and go on with it.

I cross the street and go to the building. They have an intercom at the door. Just for kicks, I look at the name of the resident in apartment forty-one. "Smith, J.," it says. Of course.

Using the key, I open the door. While I walk to the elevator, something occurs to me: if someone is there, they're probably facing the elevator. I decide to take the stairs instead.

When I reach the fourth floor, I open the door slowly. I peek inside the hallway, expecting to see a witch with guns in both hands ready to take me down.

But no one's there. I chuckle to myself. I've climbed up four floors for nothing. I glance wistfully at the elevator in the middle of the hallway. But when I'm about to step into the hallway, something catches my eye. Above the elevator doors, a plastic thingamabob seems out of place.

It's a tiny wireless camera. They *do* have her apartment under surveillance.

Unless the camera has a panoramic lens, it shouldn't have detected me. I slowly close the door to the stairs and rush down. I stop on the third floor and sneak a peek: no camera there. No camera on the second one either. They're definitely waiting for Jane.

I cross the street back to the gelato shop, looking over my shoulder. I tell the news to Jane when I'm back at the table.

"This means it's no use waiting here for someone to follow." She lets out a deep sigh. "What a wasted day."

Something's up. "Jane, what's going on?"

She still has a glazed stare.

"Jane?"

"I'm tired, Drake." Her voice cracks a little.

I don't know what to say. Jane's tough girl façade has shown some cracks before. Right before she drugged me and kissed me, she was genuinely vulnerable. When she showed up at my doorstep, bleeding and asking for help, it looked like she wasn't wearing any mask.

I do the unthinkable: I put my hand over hers, already expecting her to recoil and make a snide remark. Instead, she closes her hand around mine.

She looks at me. Her lips are curved downward. All her steely determination is gone.

Still not knowing what to say, I give her a reassuring smile.

"I need to go," she says. But she doesn't let go of my hand.

How do you cheer up someone like Jane?

"Come on, Jane. Let's get a beer somewhere. We're always doing illegal things anyway." I'm only half-joking.

She chuckles. "It's not illegal for me anymore." Jane stands up.

"What do you mean?"

"I'm twenty-one. Today."

In the time it takes me to understand what she's saying, she turns and starts to walk to the door.

"Jane, wait!"

She stops but says, "Drake. Don't."

"Come on. It's your birthday. Let's celebrate. Let's... go to a pub."

Her head shakes slightly. "There's nothing to celebrate."

"I'm serious."

She puts her hand on my shoulder. "I know. You're sweet—and I never use this word. But it's okay. I mean it: I want to be alone. I'm used to it."

Then she turns and leaves.

Chapter 10: Skye

After my talk with Connor, I go back to bed, but I can't sleep. It's a relief to have closure on that side of our relationship. And I believe that our newfound friendship will be sincere and long-lasting.

However, he needs to know the truth about the Singularity, and I'm still refusing to tell him.

I lay in my bed, and thoughts of Connor are replaced by thoughts of Drake. I can't believe that he betrayed me. We had talked, and I had clearly told him he shouldn't try using Mona to help Boulder. Drake went ahead anyway, behind my back.

It's not only the ultimate result of that—my coven kicking me out—what keeps me awake. Of course being banished will be catastrophic for me, but it was a risk I had decided to take when I hid Mona's identity.

The three things that are eating me alive will have fewer practical consequences, but they are paramount. One, it will be my lips uttering the words that will seal Mona's destiny. Two, it makes me mad that my sacrifice so far will be in vain. And, finally, the most important one: he broke my trust.

I thought I had found someone I could fully believe in. Someone I'd never lie to, someone who would never lie to me. That covenant was broken. And since trust, for me, equates to love, it means that our love was broken too.

With Drake, I thought I had found what my relationship with Connor lacked. It turns out that there are several ways to have your heart shattered.

It's not sadness that keeps me awake, though, it's pure anger. At myself, for failing to see Drake's intent. At the covens, for being so inflexible. At the Night covens, who will never stop pursuing Mona.

And that's my answer. Whatever limited, sheltered life Mona will have under the guard of my coven, it's still preferable to the alternative: having to live in hiding from the Night covens by herself. Now that the Night Sisters know that Brianna is not the Singularity, their witch hunt will never stop. It'll only be a matter of time before they find Mona, especially now it's clear she cannot control her powers. My coven would be able to hide and protect her for the rest of her life.

I see what Connor was trying to tell me.

I jump out of bed. It's a little past seven in the morning. After a long, hot shower, I dress for the weather. I can feel the energy sources in the library. I take a deep breath, open the door, and walk down the staircase.

Connor and Lady DeWees are in the library, having tea.

Before they can greet me, I announce, "I'm ready to talk. Now."

Lady DeWees raises her eyebrows, bemused. "It can wait a few minutes. I promised to wait for Katherine. She's on her way from Heathrow as we speak. As is Elsa Dunivant. Without Elsa, we wouldn't know if you're telling the truth."

"Okay." I let the slight pass.

"Did you eat?" Connor asks. "Let's have breakfast. You'll need some energy. It's going to be a long day."

He leads me to the kitchen, and the two of us share a silent meal. Tea, biscuits, and croissants.

I miss Seattle's coffee.

A commotion in the foyer reaches my ears. I'd recognize that trained, projected tone anywhere.

"Where's my darling?" Mum's voice echoes in the manor.

I sprint to my mother and give her a hug. I'm even smiling.

"Skye! How are you?"

I hear Lady DeWees scoff behind me.

"I'm fine," I reply. "Lady DeWees has been awfully welcoming."

"Camilla," Mum says, nodding in Lady DeWees' direction.

"Katherine." Lady DeWees returns the cold greeting.

I pull my mother aside. "Mum, I'm ready to tell the whole story," I whisper.

She looks in my eyes. "Are you sure?"

"I am."

***

Elsa Dunivant arrives twenty minutes after Mum, who is upstairs refreshing herself after her flight. Elsa's a delicate thing, not as old as I imagined her, but still skinny and frail. The butler helps her out of her coat. Her dress is an elegant turquoise silk, covering her thin arms, and she holds a tiny silver purse. She smiles when she sees me.

"Oh, Skye! Come here, dear, give me a hug. Goddess, look at you. We both have such rare Charms. I was hoping to meet you someday. Well, under different circumstances, of course."

Her sweetness disarms me. That's not how I pictured an interrogator.

"It's nice to finally meet you," I say.

"That's such a nice compliment. And I *know* you're being

sincere." She taps her finger to the tip of my nose in a playful way.

"How was your trip, Elsa?" Lady DeWees' voice is cold. Maybe she's upset about seeing me so chummy with my interviewer.

"Oh, the airport security line took forever. I wish we could still fly on broomsticks." Ms. Dunivant winks at me.

Connor and I chuckle.

Lady DeWees doesn't seem amused. "Please take your time to settle in, Elsa. We'll start when you're ready."

Fifteen minutes later, we're crowding the drawing room. Connor, Mum, and I stand in a corner. Lady DeWees, Ms. Dunivant, and two other Mothers are talking amongst themselves. Lady DeWees' daughter, a stunning twenty-something lawyer named Mary, is taking notes. With so many witches around me, my True Sight is buzzing like crazy. It feels like I've been hit with a stun gun.

Mary, much like Vanessa had in my last deposition, goes over the date, time, context, and participants. Then Ms. Dunivant takes over.

"Skye, my dear. Please remember that you're among friends and Sisters. We are not here to assign blame or punish you. We just want to know what you know and clarify any questions you might have. Do you trust me?"

"I trust *you*, Ms. Dunivant." I hope Mary doesn't transcribe that inflection on "you."

She chuckles. "That's the spirit. Please, call me Elsa. Now, do you know who the real Singularity is?"

"Yes."

"Who is she?"

"Mona Hunter." There, it's out. Please forgive me, Mona.

Elsa looks at the room, inquisitively.

Connor speaks up, "Mona? Is that your boyfriend's sister?"

I nod.

Elsa's eyebrows go up. "Is that why you hid her true identity? You were trying to protect her and your boyfriend?"

"*Ex*-boyfriend," I say. Curse her Truth Charm. "His name's Drake. And yes, I protected her in part because I knew him, but also because I was afraid of what would become of her if the covens got her."

"What did you think would—or will—become of her?"

"I thought she'd be taken. She'd have to live in hiding so she couldn't break the Veil. She could even become a prisoner."

"That's far-fetched," Lady DeWees interrupts.

"A prisoner. Like I've been for the past couple of days." I stare at Lady DeWees.

"Nonsense!" one of the Mothers says.

"Please, Sisters." Elsa's voice loses the sweetness and becomes commanding. "I am having a conversation with Skye. You should restrain yourselves, unless you are asked a question. Now, Skye, my dear…" She raises her eyebrows. "Connor, what are you doing?"

"I'm calling Seattle," he answers, his phone glued to his ear. "We need to secure the girl—"

Elsa interrupts him. "Goddess, boy, hold your horses! Let's be civilized and finish this before any one of us does something harsh. We need to hear the whole story."

Connor opens his mouth to protest, but Elsa's stare silences him. He sulkily turns off his phone and sits down again.

"Skye, how can you be sure this girl is the Singularity?" Elsa's voice is soft again.

"I saw her create a blaze that destroyed our school. And I *felt* her energy. We were right; she carries with her much more energy than any other Sister. I'm in a room full of Mothers, and the sum of our energies pales in comparison to hers." My voice is low. "It's amazing."

All eyes are trained on me now. They thirst for more details.

"Why didn't we find her before?"

"Because she just turned fifteen. Her Daybreak caused Seattle's earthquake a few weeks ago. The magical energy felt two years ago was just a pre-release, something only the Singularity's energy would trigger. We couldn't find her because we were looking for someone who was supposed to be seventeen now."

The Mothers exchange glances.

"Did the Night covens know about her identity?" Elsa asks.

"They suspected Brianna wasn't the Singularity. A Night Sister, Miranda, abducted me and hinted at that."

Mum can't contain herself. "What? You never said anything!"

I cast my eyes down. "If I did, you'd know they had doubts, and you would investigate it too. But I didn't tell them anything. Not that it matters now: after that huge green wave of light, I'm pretty sure they're searching for the real one."

No one asks about Jason; they have no reason to. And I have no motive to volunteer the information.

Elsa turns to Connor. "Okay, I think that's sufficient for now. You can make your calls." To Mary, she says, "Let it be known that Skye was under the Truth Charm the whole time. I certify that all she said is true to the best of her knowledge." She taps my hand affectionately. "You did well. Thank you."

Well, I really didn't have a choice, but I'm grateful for her words.

Everyone seems to be on their cell phones, but Lady DeWees commands, "Sisters, let's be careful with this information. Connor will call a couple of *trusted* Sisters in Seattle and proceed to localize and isolate the girl. Besides them, only Mothers should know the Singularity's identity."

I don't like how she scowls at me when she says the word "trusted."

Mum comes over and holds my hands. "Were you hurt when they took you?"

"Only a little," I say. In truth, it was the beating of a lifetime. But it's not Ms. Dunivant asking. "I'm just glad this is over."

Lady DeWees overhears me. She approaches and says, "But it isn't. There's still the small matter of your trial."

Mum steps between us. "Trial? Elsa said we weren't here today to assign blame."

"Not today. Today we were collecting the information Skye was supposed to have delivered a long time ago. But she must answer for withholding the information, lying to the covens, endangering the Veil, and betraying her Sisters."

"This is unacceptable," Mum says. "Come on, Skye. Let's go home." She grabs my hand.

One of the guards blocks our way. "I'm sorry, Madam."

Behind us, Lady DeWees says, "I believe Skye will be my guest for a while longer."

Chapter 11: Drake

I drive home, still feeling guilty that I didn't go after Jane. No matter who you are, spending your birthday alone is a rotten deal. But she made her wishes clear. I know little about her, but I'm sure she wouldn't play victim just to get some sympathy.

It makes me reflect on my own loneliness. Skye is gone, and I'm in the midst of a mess with Mona and all the witches. And now my mother. All these people are in my life, and I'm in theirs. Even though it's not smooth sailing all the time, what's important is that we have one another. We may do dumb things from time to time, but it's *our* dumb things.

As soon as I open the front door, I yell, "Mona, I'm home!" She made me promise to always announce my presence. I scared her out of her tights a couple of times just by being quiet.

"We're upstairs," she yells back.

I wonder who "we" is. Probably Mona and Pain. I make a smoothie with banana, honey, and the leftover kale.

While I drink it, my phone buzzes. Dad texts me that he'll be late home from work again. Maybe Mona would agree to split a pizza.

Heavy feet march down the stairs. It's Pain.

"Hey, Drake." She waves from the bottom of the stairs. She's super shy. Even with her attitude, her size—she's almost as tall as I am—and the green streaks in her hair, she looks like an oversized, awkward kid.

"Hey," I say.

She isn't ecstatic, but she isn't devastated either. I have no idea if they talked about the kiss and all that stuff. The thought gives me pause. It's weird seeing a family friend as a potential in-law all of a sudden.

"Mona was telling me about the covens' crapfest," she says. "That you may have to run away. And that your mother came back."

"Yeah. We're all shocked about that."

She nods. "Let me know if I can help. I mean, I already told Mona that. But I'm telling you too."

"Okay," I say. I'm not sure where she's going with that. "Thanks, Pain. I mean it."

Pain gives me a shy shrug, as if saying "no probs." She opens the door and leaves in a hurry.

That was weird. Well, it's always like that with Pain. But this was *weirder*.

"Mona!" I shout.

"Whaaaat?" Mona screams.

We have never learned to use our inside voices. I scoff and rush up the stairs. When I'm at her door, I ask, "Did you upset Pain?"

"Why, did she look upset?" Mona seems concerned.

"She seemed out of sorts."

Mona hugs a pillow and plops down on her bed. "Do I have to talk about this with you?"

"We'd better talk. Do we have to have some signal now? Like a tie on the front door or something?"

Her eyes narrow. "What do you m… Ew, Drake! Gross."

"I don't know if it's gross because I don't know what the deal with you two is!"

"It's nothing like that," she says. "We're not a couple, okay? We talked about it."

I take a sip of my smoothie. "Bad timing on her part, huh? Kissing you when you have all those problems."

"Don't be harsh on her, Drake. Pain was massively worried about me. She told me the kiss wasn't planned or anything; she was just relieved to see me unharmed. She even apologized for it." Mona sighs.

This is not the kind of conversation I should be having with my sister. But the one who she should talk to is Pain. Or Skye. I'm not the best option, but I'm the only option available. "And?" I ask.

"Ugh, it's horrible being in that position." She punches the mattress. "I didn't let her down, if that's what you're asking. I told her that with all that's going on—the covens and that *woman* showing up—I can't think of it right now."

"But... have you?"

"Of course. How can you not think about it?" Her voice softens. "I like Pain, only not that way. But I don't want to lose her. She's the best friend I'll ever have."

It's hard for a big brother to admit it, but Mona is stronger than I give her credit for. "That sucks. For both of you."

"I know." She grunts and buries her head in the pillow. "And I know I have to tell her sometime, but first I have to deal with everything else." Her voice is muffled.

"Are you?" I ask tentatively.

"Am I what?"

"Going to deal with everything else. Are you going to meet

Patricia?"

She resurfaces from the pillow. Her eyebrows are pinched. "Who?"

"Our mother, Mona."

"Ugh. No. I just want her to crawl back to wherever the hell she came from," she hisses.

I want to talk more about Patricia. I get why Mona feels this way, but she can't hide forever from her mother. But I decide that we've done enough sibling bonding for one night. I let it go.

"Dad is late again," I tell her.

She sighs. "Pizza?"

Chapter 12: Skye

Mum and I are about to protest Lady DeWees' decision to maintain me as a captive, but Connor enters the foyer. He is ashen. "Something has happened. Vanessa is dead."

It takes me a second to place the name. "The girl who interviewed me?"

Connor nods. He looks devastated. "Yes. She was one of the two witches helping me coordinate the Search. I contacted the other, Rhonda. When Rhonda showed up at my flat in Seattle, the police were there. They found no immediate cause of death, but there were signs of a struggle. And now the Seattle police want to talk to me." He keeps turning the phone in his hand.

"Connor, I'm so sorry," I whisper.

Lady DeWees and Mum also offer him their sympathies.

Connor shakes his head. He looks weary. "Do you think it was the Night covens?"

"They might be desperate looking for the Singularity," I say. "Miranda is ruthless, and she has a witch assassin working for her."

Lady DeWees is indignant. "Why didn't you tell us? Are you actively sabotaging—"

"Oh, Goddess, don't pin this on me!" I snap. "I'm trying to help."

This shuts her up.

"I have to go to Seattle," Connor says. "I need to clear this up with the police and organize things. Rhonda is in a panic, and we need to get the Singularity soon. Please tell Nigel I'm going to pack. I'll be ready to go to Heathrow in five minutes."

Mum steps away and makes a call while Connor climbs the steps to pack. I follow him into his guest bedroom.

While he shoves his clothes into his luggage, I ask, "Are you okay?"

"I… I don't know what to say to her family. I know them. I convinced them to let her help me."

"Were you close?"

"Yes. Well, not like that. I was hosting her in my flat while I came here. There's nothing between us. She even has a fiancé." Connor pauses. "Goddess! What am I going to tell *him*?"

I clutch his arm gently. "Do you want to me go with you?"

He resumes his packing. "I don't think Lady DeWees would let you leave. Do you think…? Do you think if you called Mona, she would hide and wait for our Sisters to pick her up?"

There it is. It's almost like he's testing me. He's dangling in front of me an opportunity to help or hinder the Search.

"If I called Mona, she would hide *from* us. She would tell Drake, and they would flee."

Connor stares at me, as if making sure I'm sincere. "When we get her, I'll do my best to make sure she lives a normal life. At least, as normal as it can be."

He zips up his Portofino bag, and we go downstairs.

All the Mothers are in the foyer discussing the shocking news. Connor stops a couple of steps shy of the ground floor. "I just want to say one thing," he says. They turn their attention to him. "I'll clean up this mess and get Mona Hunter. It may take a while. But you will not put Skye on trial in my absence."

Lady DeWees says, "It's nice of you to want to attend your friend's—"

"I won't just be attending. I'll be testifying in her defense." He leans toward me and says, "Take care."

After Connor leaves, Mum and Lady DeWees go to the drawing room to discuss my "temporary housing situation." I sneak into Connor's guest room and try the landline phone. Dead. Hm.

***

I hear Mum climbing the steps. I reach my room before she does and pretend I'm folding my clothes.

"How are you, darling?" she asks.

I drop my stuff on the bed and hug her. It's been such a long time! "I missed you," I say.

"I missed you too," she whispers while stroking my hair.

We sit on the bed. "I'm sorry I lied to you."

"As long as you had a good reason."

"I did! At least, I thought I did."

I tell her the whole story up until I hid Mona. But I omit everything about Jane showing up after the fire. I also hide details of my kidnapping by the Night covens. I know my mother. She would never let me leave home again if she knew.

***

A knock on the open door startles me. Elsa is there.

"Elsa. I thought the interrogation was over." My mother is not amused.

"It is, Katherine. It is. I only have a couple of questions. For

Skye's benefit."

"Please forgive me for being skeptical," Mum replies.

Elsa ignores her. "Skye, was one of the reasons for hiding the girl your love for your lad?"

"No," I say. Wow.

"But do you love him?"

"I do," I reply. Wait, what?

"Thank you, dear," Elsa says.

Mum asks her, "Is that all you needed to know?"

She chuckles. "Oh, it wasn't *me* who needed to know it."

Elsa winks at me and leaves.

Chapter 13: Drake

The last few days were crazy, even for my witch-heavy standards.

However, today has been a normal day. After school I had swim practice and stayed longer for a few laps by myself. I'm centered now. I finish my shower and leave the locker room feeling relaxed.

I drive home with the classic rock radio station blasting from the speakers. My brain still refuses to engage in any complex problems. In my own personal fantasy, this is a day like any other.

When I arrive home, Dad comes to the door. Uh-oh.

"Okay, don't freak out, buddy. You have another visitor."

"I thought people only had one mother," I say.

"It's Skye's aunt."

Aunt Gemma rises from the couch when I come in. She's wearing her usual denim jacket, t-shirt, and jeans, yet her appearance is different. Instead of the scowling expression she has always greeted me with, she shows a worried face.

"Is Skye okay?" I ask.

"Yes! Uh, no, because she's being... held in London for a while."

This time, Dad doesn't leave. He's as curious as I am. "Did she ask you to come here?"

"Her mother did. Katherine didn't want to contact you directly because, you know, the phones."

Dad frowns.

"Sure," I say in an upbeat mode, failing epically to disguise the tension. "What's the message?"

Aunt Gemma sneaks a peek to Dad before replying, "They know about Mona."

"What are you talking about? They know *what* about Mona?" Dad demands.

She freezes. Aunt Gemma is not sure how much Dad knows, and she seems terrified of breaking the Veil.

But it's too late now. It's time for my father to share my grief and wonderment.

"Dad, listen to me. A lot of things are going to happen in the next few hours. Messed up stuff. Get your phone and call Patricia right now."

"Why? What's going on?"

"Please, just do it."

He hesitates, but leaves to get his phone from the office.

While he's away, I ask Gemma. "Who knows?"

"For now, just the London Mothers. But a Sister here was found dead."

My heart sinks. "Who?" Images of Yara, Greta, and even Jane swirl in my head.

"Vanessa. A girl visiting from Oregon. You don't know her. They think the Night covens must be conducting their own witch hunt."

I caused this. My stunt with Boulder's cure triggered the green wave that alerted the Night covens. It saved Boulder, but it condemned this girl. And maybe more people. Maybe Mona.

Dad gets back, and I snatch the phone from him. "Patricia? It's Drake. The covens know about Mona, and the Night sisters are

79

starting to kill suspects."

It takes only a second, but she is calm and composed. Maybe it's the assassin training kicking in. "What do you need?"

"First of all, I need you to meet with Dad and explain it to him. Mona and I will run and hide. When we're safe, I'll call you from my phone and let you know our location. Then you can pick up Mona."

"Okay," she says. Once again, in control of her emotions. "Put your father on the phone."

Dad's jaw is open, but he accepts the phone and brings it to his ear. "Yeah?" he says to Patricia.

"Mona!" I yell.

"Whaaat?" she yells back from her room.

"Come here!"

"You come here!"

"Mona!"

Dad puts his finger in his other ear. Mona stomps down the stairs.

"What?" she asks when she appears halfway down. She looks at Gemma with curiosity.

"Get your amulet and your potions. We need to leave," I say.

Mona's eyes go wide. She looks at Dad, at Gemma, and at me in turns until she makes the connection.

"*Now* would be awesome," I add.

She leaves in a hurry for her room. Dad ambles to the kitchen, still on the phone with Patricia.

"Thanks, Aunt Gemma," I say. "But why is Katherine warning us? I thought the Mothers wanted Mona for themselves."

Aunt Gemma shakes her head. But what she says shakes me. "I don't know. Maybe they worry the Night Sisters might get her first."

Dad comes back from the kitchen. "Drake, tell me right now what's going on." His eyes are narrowed, his voice angry. The ever-worried Dad has been replaced by a much fiercer, much steelier man.

"Dad, Patricia will tell you in detail. The most important thing right now is keeping Mona away from here."

"Why did Patricia ask me to not call the police?" He growls.

"She's right. It would take days to explain it to the police, and by then it might be too late."

"But Patricia can explain it to me?"

I sigh. Here it comes. "Yes, Dad. You don't remember, but once you told me that Patricia was a witch. And she was. She is. And so is Mona."

"Drake…" But he doesn't go on. He knows it's not that far-fetched. He believed in it once. No doubt his brain is connecting the dots.

"Dad, please trust me."

He stares at me, and then he nods.

The stomping on the stairs resumes. "I'm ready!" Mona announces. She has a backpack slung over her shoulder.

Mona kisses Dad on the cheek.

I give him a hug. "I'll keep you and Patricia posted," I say. "Do not call me on my phone under any circumstances. Patricia has my secret number. You should have it too." I get his phone from him and add the number to his contacts.

Dad nods, speechless, and hands us a wad of cash. He turns to Gemma. "I have to leave and meet with Patricia. I'll give you a ride home."

I look through the living room window, but I only see cars I recognize from the neighborhood. "We're clear," I announce.

I take off with Mona in my car, while Dad and Gemma drive away in the opposite direction.

"Where are we going?" Mona asks.

Good question. For now, I'm going around Green Lake Park. It can't be any of the witch homes, so the houses of Yara and Greta are out of the question. I consider choosing one of Jane's empty places—the house in North Seattle or the apartment in Fremont— but I remember the camera above the elevator. The Night covens are monitoring them to catch Jane. I'm at a loss. We can't drop by Priscilla's or Sean's without a good explanation. And Boulder's house is not an option.

"Too bad we can't stay with Pain," I say. "She's your best friend. I'm sure they'll show up there sooner or later."

"Pain's family has an old house in Lake Stevens. They used to rent it, but it's empty now. We went there a couple of times."

"That would work! Do you know the address?"

"I know how to get there. And where they keep the key."

Things are looking up. "Awesome. We'll go there." I leave Green Lake Way and enter Aurora Avenue. We need to take I-5 North. "We'll give Patricia a couple of hours to talk things over with Dad, and then we'll call her so she can pick you up."

Mona slaps me on the top of my head. "Don't be dumb!"

"What was that for?"

Mona looks at me as if I'm the crazy one. "I'm not going to stay with that woman. She comes out of nowhere after thirteen years, and now I'm supposed to trust her? To stay with her? No way."

"We need someone who can protect you, who can take you away if the covens close in. I can't do it. Dad gave me some money, but we'll run out soon. We're both minors. Patricia has the resources and knows how to hide. Also, she looks like you. She might even use her real identity and prove you're her daughter."

"I'm not her daughter!" Mona slaps the armrest. "I'll stay with Jane. She needs me to rescue Jason anyway."

I want to pull over to look Mona in the eyes while we have this conversation, but I don't want to attract attention to us. Not many cars drive on Aurora Avenue that late at night.

"You don't want to stay with your mother, but you'll stay with the girl who tried to kill you?"

"Jane saved me a few days ago. She brought me back to you. And she's good at survival. I know what to expect from Jane. But Patricia… I don't even know her. She may be a murderer for all I know."

I forget the road and stare at Mona.

"What?" she asks.

"You know, you may have an Intuition Charm, just like Jane."

"What do you mean?"

It's a forty-minute drive to our destination. Plenty of time for me to tell Mona that our mother is indeed an assassin, and all the other tidbits from my meeting with her.

***

After I tell the whole story, Mona doesn't speak. We're near Lake Stevens. She and I focus on finding the correct house. It's a well-maintained old rambler a couple of blocks from the lake. We park in the back. Mona fetches the key from under a black rock.

We enter and turn on the lights. The house is freezing. I crank up the thermostat while Mona looks in the fridge.

"It's empty," she says.

"Are you hungry? I can get something from the 7-Eleven."

"No, it's okay." She sits on the couch, her head down.

I sit by her side. "What do you think?"

"About our mother being an assassin? Awesome."

"Well, she wants to do the right thing. Help us. Protect us. And she had a hell of a reason to stay away. Did I change your mind?"

She shakes her head. "At least with Jane I know what the deal is."

I chuckle. "Skye would freak out if she knew you chose Jane over your mother."

"Skye talked, didn't she? That's how her coven knows."

"They had a witch with a Truth Charm. Skye had no option. She's the one who tried to hide you in the first place."

"I know, I know. I wish she had figured out a way of lying to them." Mona's voice is not angry, only tired.

"Should I call Jane?"

Mona nods. I use the burner phone Jane gave to me to call my former enemy. Well, at least I hope the "former" part is true.

"Hey, Drake."

I put her on speakerphone. "Jane, we're in trouble. The London covens know about Mona. We need to hide her. I have the place, but I have no idea what to do."

"You got a place? Is it safe? Were you followed?" Jane's directness is somewhat reassuring. She thinks things through.

"No one followed us. No one knows we're here."

"Give me the address."

***

Mona caves in, and I make a quick run to the convenience store. I get a coffee for me and a hot chocolate for her, plus chips, beef jerky, a box of cookies, and two bottles of water.

"Is that what athletes eat?" Mona asks when I get back.

84

"When they're on the run."

She smirks.

Right after we finish our snack, we hear a motorcycle engine. For a moment, I fear that it might be Scythe, the witch assassin who almost kidnapped Mona. What's up with the Night witches and their bikes?

But the knock on the door is accompanied by Jane's voice. "It's me."

I open the door and let her in. Jane comes inside, nods to me, and gives Mona a quick hug. I stare at our leather-clad new companion.

"What?" Jane asks.

"I didn't peg you as the hugging kind."

Jane rolls her eyes. "Oh, the things you don't know…"

"I'm glad you came," I say, trying to atone for my comment.

"What's going on?" Jane's tunnel vision is back; her hugging demeanor is already forgotten.

We tell her about Aunt Gemma's warning and Vanessa's death.

Jane frowns. "Isn't this woman a Knowing helping the London covens? Why would she warn you?"

"She thinks the Night covens are hunting and killing any witches. Or, at least, Skye's mother thinks that," I say.

"Hey, Jane," Mona says. "I will help you with Jason."

Jane smiles for the first time. She relaxes and sits in the sofa. "Because you're desperate?"

"We're desperate, but we have options. Mona is the one who doesn't want to go with our mother," I tell Jane.

"Why would you trust a Mother? They're after you."

"Not *a* Mother. *My* mother! My mommy," I say. I haven't used that last word for years.

That gives Jane some pause. "You're full of surprises, aren't you?"

I shrug. "More like the women around me."

"So your mother is back from... wherever. Is this related to Mona's secret?"

Mona says, "Yes. She came out of nowhere claiming she wants to help me run away. Don't you think that's suspicious? I'm going with you."

I pull a chair up and sit in front of Mona. "Do you have a plan?"

"I haven't got it all set up yet. I wasn't expecting that Mona would be exposed so soon. The Night covens know all my usual places. I've been hiding for the last few days, changing motels every night. Can we stay here? It's close to Seattle, but the houses are so far apart I don't think we'll run into another Sister here."

"Pain's family doesn't use this house often. But the neighbors might call if they see movement and lights," Mona says.

I think about it. "I'll meet Pain and tell her you're here. If her parents ask, she can say she offered the cabin to you for a few days. She'll be concerned about you anyway."

Jane is shaking her head. "No, don't tell her. Let's take this risk. One thing you geniuses might not have considered: when Mona doesn't show up for school tomorrow, the covens will know you fled. They'll go after you, Drake. And this Pain girl. You can't tell anyone where we are. And if Miranda is keeping an eye on your family, she'll know too." Jane leans forward. "I was hoping to use Skye's True Sight to find Jason, but now I'll have to do it by myself."

"I can help," Mona insists.

"Okay. Let's do this," Jane says, looking at me with expectant eyes. "Agreed?"

It's time to trust her with no reservations. "Right."

Jane nods. She fishes a flask from her leather jacket. "Here. Leave. Get onto I-five, drive for ten minutes. Then pull over at a gas station and drink this."

This is odd, even for Jane. "Do you want to score me a DUI? What's this?"

"Forget Potion. If the covens find you, you need to have total deniability. Drink it all."

"How far back does it go?" No one can blame me for being suspicious. Jane has tricked me with potions before.

"A few hours. It's potent, but a potion going further back may do you damage. You will still know that Mona is with me—we discussed that days ago. But you won't know where. Come on. Drink it."

"Sure." Why argue? Crazy is my new normal.

***

The fluorescent light of the convenience store fascinates me. Its buzzing sound is hypnotic. I look back to the shelves. Ooh, Doritos!

I grab a bag and a soda and walk to the cashier. After I pay, I ask, "Is this Mill Creek?"

The attendant looks at me funny. "Yep."

I nod. I have been here before. Dad was driving us to Vancouver, but we left low on gas and stopped here to fill up. But I can't remember why I'm here. Or *how* I ended up here.

I sit in the car for a couple of minutes. I remember Skye's aunt went to my house and warned us to run away. Then… what? Did I leave with Mona?

My burner phone rings. I pick up.

"Drake?"

"Hey, Jane." Maybe she can help me. "The weirdest—"

"Did you drink it yet?"

I look around the gas station. Is she following me? "No, I just bought it." I stare at the soda can.

Jane chuckles. "Did you buy a drink? It makes sense. The potion makes you thirsty. Listen, you just drank a Forget potion. You left Mona with me, and we vanished. She's safe. That's all you need to know."

"Hold on…"

"I didn't want you to freak out when you figured Mona is gone. Now, remember: do *not* go home. They may be watching. Disappear. Be clueless."

"That should be easy," I mumble.

Jane hangs up.

I call Patricia. She tells me where she and Dad are: in a motel south of Seattle. I drive there, trying to piece together the last few hours, to no avail. The only thing I accomplish is getting my steering wheel dirty with orange Doritos dust.

***

"Drake, she's a kid! I can't let her run away!"

"Dad, calm down." We're in Patricia's motel room, and I'm afraid the other guests will call the police. That's the last thing we need. "She's safe."

He sits down on the bed with his head in his hands.

Patricia occupies a wobbly chair by the bathroom door. She's giving him some time.

My father looks at me. "I can't understand. You're telling me that my Mona caused an earthquake?"

I nod. "And the school fire. Oh, and the house fire."

Patricia can't control herself. "House fire?"

"A few years back. It's was kind a pre-Daybreak release of magical energy," I explain.

"This is too dangerous!" Dad is still restless.

"Not to her. She's immune to fire," I say.

This time, both of them look at me wide-eyed. I need to learn to temper my statements.

I pat Dad's back. "I know this is a lot to take in all at once. I learned about all of this in the space of months, and I'm shaken. You do understand that Mona, Skye, and Patricia are honest to goodness witches, right? You already knew something was up; you told me once."

"I was rambling. I suspected something, but I never took it seriously. But Patricia proved it to me before you came."

I raise my eyebrows. My curiosity is killing me, but I don't want to derail this delicate convo. "Good. And you realize that Mona is this freakishly powerful witch. This is not going away. She can't get rid of this gift. The bad guys want to get her and use her magic; the good guys want to protect her, but she must hide for the rest of her life."

He shoots me a vacant stare. "But you and Mona are my babies, buddy." His voice is choked. "You're my kids. I can't let them hurt you. I can't let anyone take you away from me."

I hug my father. Behind him, I see Patricia wiping her wet eyes. "It's all right, Dad."

He hugs me back, tight. Then he lets me go, and a focused expression takes over his face. "Okay, I accept that this crazy thing is happening. I don't understand it completely, but I get that these people are after Mona. Now, what are our options?"

I'm amazed at his quick turnaround. Dad is always worried, but when a real crisis emerges, his practical side takes over. I take a deep breath. "The way I see it, we have few options."

"Go on," Dad encourages me.

"We can't let the Night covens near Mona under any circumstance." I remember how they kidnapped Skye and killed the Vanessa girl, but I don't mention that to Dad. "We could run, and keep running all our lives. But we don't have magic, only Mona does. And if she uses hers, she might cause another disaster and alert all witches from both sides. Then we would be back to square one."

Dad nods. "Or?"

"Or we could hand her over to the good covens. Skye's people. They would hide her and protect her with their lives; I'm certain of it. But Mona would be gone from us, Dad. Actually, you and I may have to flee anyway, so the Night covens don't get us and use us against her."

"What you're telling me is that Mona's life will be over, one way or another." He stands up, his hands balled into fists, and starts pacing the room. "This is too much to absorb, Drake. This is a decision I can't make lightly."

"Ben," Patricia says is a gentle voice. "Mona could come with me. As you know—and I'm sorry to say that—I'm good at hiding. But you're right, Mona would spend her whole life looking over her shoulder. This is not a good life. Trust me."

He looks at her, his eyes narrowed. He shakes his head. "I don't think we have an option, buddy. Mona should go with the good guys, for her own sake. You and I will figure out something."

"Drake, can you go back and bring us Mona?" She says.

I look down. "Er, no. I don't know where she is."

"Drake!" Dad growls.

"I can call her!" I say. "She's with Jane, a witch I trust. But first I need to contact the good guys."

Chapter 14: Skye

The tingling that signals a Sister approaching awakens me. Mum knocks on my door and comes into the room.

"Good morning, darling. How are you doing?"

I stretch and let out a long, loud yawn, not appropriate for a lady, but very much appropriate for my restless night of sleep.

Mum chuckles. "Okay, I'll give you a minute."

What is she doing up so early? She is a fervent believer in beauty rest. Sometimes she doesn't see morning daylight for weeks in a row.

"You're upbeat this morning," I mumble. "And awake."

She raises her eyebrows. "Time is of the essence now, Skye."

Mum never stops acting. She can't leave the theatre. Sometimes she speaks in riddles, like those stereotypical old wise-men in plays. Half-truths, half-sentences, weird word emphasis: those are all part of her arsenal. But, this time, she seems to be doing it on purpose.

"Connor should arrive in Seattle soon," she says. "He'll go to the police right away to give a deposition about the young lady's passing, but he has already stationed a surveillance team at Drake's house."

"What are they going to do?"

"They'll just observe until Connor joins them. Then he has a plan to take her in."

I jump out of bed. "I should be there! Mona is going to freak out if they ambush her. She may cause another fire or earthquake—"

"Connor is smart, Skye. Now he knows what she's capable of doing. He'll be careful. And he won't hurt her."

I pace the bedroom. "This is not right. I can help. Can't I go there until the trial?"

Mum lowers her eyes. "That's the thing I came to tell you. They want to do the audience right away. I tried to dissuade Lady DeWees, but she stood her ground. She thinks every minute that this situation is not resolved, we endanger the Veil."

"And, by 'resolving the situation,' she means kicking me out of the covens."

Mum puts her hand on my arm. "We won't let that happen."

"What can we do?"

Mum smiles one of those stage-crafted mysterious grins. There she is, the oracle who can only spout enigmas.

"Mum!"

"I have a plan."

My True Sight buzzes. "Someone is coming."

Mary shows up at the door. "Connor is on the phone. He wants to talk to you in the library."

We all go down after her. I'm still in my pajamas, but I don't care.

Lady DeWees is already waiting for us in the library. "We're all here," she says.

Connor's voice on the loudspeaker is clear, "I've got bad news. Vanessa was murdered by a Night Sister. The police think she was poisoned. They can't figure out the chemical, but I saw the dart and the reports; it's clearly a potion. And they're after me."

"Oh, no," I blurt out. "Connor, it's Skye. How do you know?"

"They left a message. Listen, Sisters. This is getting out of control.

92

The Night covens aren't hiding anymore. They're after us, and they won't stop until they get the Singularity."

Lady DeWees asks, "Are they going to break the Veil?"

"I don't think they care about the Veil anymore," he answers. "I just left the police station. Here's my plan. I'll alert all the Sisters and witch families in the area. All Sisters that need extra protection will get assigned a witch or a Knowing bodyguard. I can move some guards from the hospital now. And I'm organizing a group to go to Mona's house. We need to talk to her and move her somewhere safe before we can bring her to London."

I can't keep quiet. "This is not going to work! When she's agitated, she can't control her magic. You might create another disaster."

"I thought about that, Skye. I need you to call her and talk to her… and to your boyfriend." His voice is a growl. "Calm them down. Tell them it's in their best interests to collaborate with us."

All eyes in the room are on me now. "I don't know if they'll listen to me," I say. "They're pretty strong-headed."

"Skye, you need to make them see it's over," Connor says. "In the end, Mona's options are either the Night Sisters or us. If she ends up alive."

"I'll do my best."

"Make it happen," he commands. "Time's up."

***

I created this situation. I hid Mona from my coven. Now Vanessa is dead, and my Sisters are in danger. It's all my responsibility. All my fault.

I can never undo what's been done, but I can try to fix it.

"Make the call," Lady DeWees says to me.

93

"It's better if I do it alone."

"I'm not sure we can trust you," she replies.

"What?" Mum says. "She volunteered the girl's name! She hasn't been anything but helpful since she arrived here."

"Exactly," Lady DeWees says. "*Since she arrived here.* The months before, not so much."

"I will convince them," I say. "They're in danger, and I care for them. But to do that, I need to be alone. I don't want you second-guessing me. I don't need *me* second-guessing me."

Lady DeWees stares at me, her lips pursed, her foot tapping on the floor. Then she walks to the door and opens it. The butler is there.

"Please make sure Miss Lexington-Ellis is not disturbed," she tells him. To the people in the room, she says, "Let's leave so she can make the call."

Mum exhales, apparently relieved. She kisses my forehead before leaving.

As soon as the door closes, I pick up the landline. This one has a signal. That's how they're keeping me incommunicado: only this phone is connected.

I don't want to waste a moment, not with breakfast, or dressing up, or any other distraction. I remind myself how to make an international call from England and dial Drake's number. It's almost eight in the morning here, so it's close to midnight in Seattle. I bet he's still awake.

"Skye!"

His voice stirs something inside me. A warmth traverses my body, but at the same time a sense of regret and sorrow washes over me. I'm not prepared for this. I take a deep breath. "Hey, you."

"I'm glad you called." He's measuring his words. I can detect the strain in his voice. "How are you? Are they treating you well?"

"Drake, listen to me. The Night covens are killing the Sisters. They won't stop until they get to you and Mona. It's over, Drake."

"I know, Aunt Gemma told me. I took care of it. How are you?" He sounds overly calm.

"What? What do you mean, Aunt Gemma? What happened? How did you take care of it?" I have so many questions, I can't prioritize them.

"It's taken care of. Don't worry. Are you all right?"

"Drake, what did you do this time?"

He waits a moment before replying, "I can't tell you on this line. Right?"

I jump up and slap the table. "It doesn't matter anymore! Connor needs to take Mona somewhere safe. She must go with him, Drake. We can't save her if she doesn't come to us."

Silence.

"Drake? Are you there? Listen to me; Mona needs to go with Connor. Please make sure she does that without destroying the block."

"This might be… problematic."

"Why? What happened?"

"I hope this line is safe. Here's the thing: Mona is with Jane. I have no idea where."

I'm not sure I'm hearing right. "Jane took her?"

"We asked Jane to stay with her. She's protecting Mona."

I can't even speak loud anymore. "Are you insane?" I whisper.

"It was Mona's decision, and I supported her. It's for the best. The only other option was Patricia, and Mona hates her."

"Who the hell is Patricia?"

"Oh. Yeah. My mother. You kind of missed that."

This makes me sit down again. I'm sweating; my heart is racing. "Damn, Drake, I'm gone a few days and you manage to make things even worse."

His voice changes. "Those were impossible choices! I could let Boulder die, or I could lie to you. How can anyone make the correct decision? At least I can apologize to you now; I couldn't apologize to my dead friend, could I? And Mona had to go either with Jane, who rescued her before, or my mother, who abandoned her and, by the way, is a witch."

I can't even process this last bit. "I shouldn't have left," I mumble.

"Yes, you shouldn't have. You blame me, but I made tough calls, and I stand by them."

"I had to make tough decisions too, Drake."

"You did. Some of these decisions involve you leaving, though."

That stings. Truth always does.

"Come on, Drake. That's not fair."

He sighs. "We should be making those decisions *together*, Skye."

"Okay, let's make one now. Do you agree that Mona is better off with us?"

"Yes. Considering the alternatives."

"Lead Connor to Mona, then. Help him, and make Mona come without freaking out."

"Okay. Let's do that."

I give him Connor's number. Drake tells me about leaving Mona with Jane and then drinking a Forget potion. We figure out they will still try to rescue Jason from Miranda.

96

"Great," I say. "Jane is leading her right to the Night covens."

"No, she's not. Jane won't do anything to put Jason at risk. Or Mona."

I have to ask. "Do you still believe she won't trade one for the other?"

"At this point, does it matter what I think? Sorry. This is all too much."

He's right. He shouldn't have to carry this burden alone. I make a snap decision. "I'm coming back."

Nothing.

"Drake. Are you there?"

"Will they let you come back?"

"I guess. I mean, if it's to help find Mona. I can convince her that they gave me a guarantee about her future."

"Okay. Let me know when you arrive, and I'll pick you up."

I was expecting a more emotional reaction, but he sounds detached. And I don't know how to finish the conversation. The "I miss you" that's lodged on my throat won't do; I don't know how he'll interpret that.

"Okay. Bye," I say.

After I hang up, I keep staring at the phone for a long time.

***

When I open the door, Mum and Lady DeWees are waiting for me in the foyer, shooting me inquisitive looks.

"I'm sorry. Mona has fled, and Drake doesn't know where she is."

"What?" Lady DeWees is not hiding her indignation.

"They… sensed something was off."

Mum averts her eyes in an admission of guilt. She is the one who told Aunt Gemma to warn them.

Lady DeWees paces the room. "How is that possible? The girl is only fifteen years old. How can she manage?"

"She's pretty resourceful. And she's with an older Sister," I say, trying to ease Lady DeWees' fears.

"Who? Ours or theirs?"

"Neither. It's Jane," I reply meekly. Before Lady DeWees' rage erupts, I add, "Yes, she's the one who tried to kill Mona once, but she's redeemed herself. Drake trusts her." I can hear how ridiculous that sounds even as the words come out of my mouth.

Lady DeWees stops in front of me. Her penetrating eyes scan my face. "I think you're lying. I think you told him to hide the girl. What was your confession? Just a cheap ploy to buy time to let her escape?"

"Camilla, that's enough!" Mum shouts. "Skye has been cooperating."

"If you don't trust me, call Elsa back," I say. "She'll confirm I'm telling the truth."

Mum raises her hand, motioning me to stop. "That won't be necessary. Right, Camilla?"

Lady DeWees' gaze flickers between Mum and me. "All right. We must warn Connor right away."

"I can do it. I need to tell him I'm coming back to help them search and convince Mona."

My hostess goes rigid again. "Absolutely not! You've caused enough damage as it is. You will stay and face the Council!"

"Camilla—" Mum says.

"Don't 'Camilla' me! Besides the trust issue, Skye, what help have you been? You botched your assignment and hid the truth from us. And a few minutes ago you told me that you could bring us the girl

98

and didn't deliver again. Why would we give you yet another chance to fail?"

"You can't stop me!"

"Of course I can. This is not a request. This is coven law."

"Now I'm being incarcerated? I thought I was a guest."

Lady DeWees sizes me up. "Not anymore."

***

Just like that, I become a prisoner. Mum protests, to no avail. Two guards stand beside my door and one other is in the backyard under the room's window. They search my room for phones and other electronic devices, and Lady DeWees herself searches *me*. I'm not to leave my bedroom under any circumstances, and I'm not allowed visitors or any contact with the outside. All my meals are brought in. Thank Goddess the bedroom is a suite.

Yes, this is all illegal. However, no Sisters, not even Mum, would dare to involve the police in this situation. Scandals, investigations, and inquests are bad for the Veil. After my arrest orders, Mum says to me, in that cryptic tone of hers, "Let it play out, darling."

It's not even the trial that anguishes me; it's the knowledge that I can help find Mona and plead with her. If Connor finds her, but botches his attempt to bring her in, it may cause destruction and the Veil could be broken.

I don't have access to the internet. I occupy my mind with old books, but I can't stop thinking. I try taking hot showers to calm down, but it doesn't work. I'm not less restless, but I must be the cleanest girl in London by now.

Chapter 15: Drake

I'm on my way to meet Yara when I receive a text from Aunt Gemma: "Skye cannot come. She's going on trial. Good luck."

All my hopes of Skye helping Mona are dashed. Not to mention my own selfish hopes.

Yara's house seems decorated by a psychedelic designer. Each room is painted in a different color. We're in the basement. In the *pink* basement.

At least now that Yara and I are on the same page, romance-wise, I feel much more comfortable around her.

"What do you need?" she asks.

"A plan."

Her shoulders slump. "You don't even know what to do? Okay, let's figure it out. What do you *want?*"

That's easy. "I want to protect Mona."

"What else? I know you want Skye back too." Yara's bluntness is simultaneously startling and refreshing.

"Yes. But let's make that a secondary goal. I want to avoid her banishment."

Yara's eyebrows narrow. "That might be harder than you getting her back. But first things first. Now, I know that Skye was getting those potions for Mona. Here's a list of what I gave Skye. Do you know if you still have those?"

I scan the list and point at a few items. "We used the Clean Slate and a Healing potion on Jane."

"On Jane? The crazy girl who tried to kill Mona and then saved her? What's her deal?"

I think it's time to trust Yara completely. I tell her about Jane's brother and her attempt to rescue him. "Jane needs Mona's help for that. And Mona wants to do it."

My regular phone rings. Priscilla. I tell Yara to excuse me for a moment.

"Hey, Pri."

"Hi, Drake. Did you go to Boulder's?"

"Yeah. He's doing much better. He looks like he'll fully recover."

"Oh, God, I hope so." The trembling in her voice worries me. "Have you talked to Skye? She's not returning my texts."

Great, yet another loose end. "She's having a family thing. I think she'll be in London for a while."

In front of me, Yara raises her eyebrows.

"Oh, no. Tell her to call me. And you keep me in the loop, okay?"

"Sure thing, Pri." I think about hanging up, but I feel bad that Skye is not here for her. "What about you? How are you holding up?"

She doesn't answer right away. I can hear her breathing hard. Finally, she says, "I'm just relieved Boulder is out of the woods."

"He's lucky to have you," I say. I mean it.

"Oh, Drake… Thanks."

"Take it easy, Pri. Catch you later."

Yara is staring at me.

"What?" I ask.

She shakes her head. "No wonder girls like you."

"What do you mean?"

She makes a dismissive gesture, like she's swatting a fly. "Never mind. Where is Mona right now?"

"I can't tell you. I really can't. I don't know. But she's safe."

Yara bites her lip. "We can buy Mona some time. I can confess that I'm the Singularity. The covens would be busy testing me and whatnot."

"What? No! That is out of the question! The Night covens would know it soon too, and you'd be in danger."

"I can take care of myself."

"No, it wouldn't work. They've been burned before with Brianna. They'd be wary of your story. Please tell me you're not doing that."

"Okay... I just want to help."

"Why are you helping me, Yara?"

She casts her eyes down. "You know why. I'm your friend. And you may not believe it, but I'm a romantic. I want to see your love story come true."

"But I haven't been your friend. I wasn't very nice to you before."

"What are you talking about? You took a bullet for me. Well, a Paralysis potion, but we both thought it was a bullet. Not many friends do that."

I smile at her. Yara is all right. I believe her when she says she wants to see Skye and me together. But Skye can't return right now. And I doubt they'll let her near Mona in the future. What if she's banished?

I can't let that happen. Even though I have a better chance of getting her back if she's kicked out of the covens, I'd be a jerk to let that happen.

My decision becomes easy.

"I've got a plan," I tell Yara.

She leans forward. "Just like that? That took you, what, four minutes?"

"Well, I didn't say it was a smart plan… For one, I need to accept I can't help Mona at this point. She's out of my hands for the moment."

"Okay. Well, if Jane is as kick-ass as you claim, your sister should be okay."

"Here's what I need." I begin explaining to her how she can help me. I make up parts of the plan as I go, usually prompted by Yara's questions. She gets out her laptop and starts typing up notes and ideas.

I hope Skye doesn't hate me for what I'm about to do.

***

Boulder is in bed, but the sight is different from my last visit. The bed is reclined a bit, and he looks much better. When he opens his mouth to greet me, I seriously get goose bumps.

"Hey," he says in a guttural voice. He even waves weakly at me.

"Hey, man," I reply. "How you feeling?"

He looks down at his bed, moving his gaze from the sheets to his arms still holding intravenous tubes. I don't know if he's trying to say "What do you think?" or if he's still having trouble controlling his eyes.

He ends up saying, "Could be worse."

I have to make an effort to understand what he's saying, so I decide to talk. I tell him about football and upcoming action movies. I don't talk about girls. His fight with Priscilla is the reason he's glued to that damn bed. But he's the one to broach the subject.

"Pri was here." He pauses and takes a deep breath. "We. Have. Been talking."

"That's great, man! I'm glad for you."

"Skye?" he asks. It's still too much effort for him to speak in full sentences.

I fill in the blanks. "She had a family emergency and left for London. I know Pri must be mad that she left again, huh?"

Boulder nods.

"I'll talk to Skye about it. Hey, may I tell you a secret?"

Boulder's eyes twinkle.

"I'm going to London to bring her back. Right now. That's why I came to visit you. I'll be there for a few days."

His smile is a little bit lopsided, but I can see the old Boulder smirk there. I can only imagine the snarky remarks he has stored in his brain but can't say.

Before I leave his room, I make him promise he won't tell anyone about my trip.

His father is waiting for me in the living room. "He's still incredibly weak," Jeff says. "He makes a tremendous effort when he has visitors. The physical therapy has started too."

It's only Jeff and I in the living room. "Does he know about… my role?"

Jeff shakes his head. "He knows you were here when he woke up. That's about it. Diana, Serena, and I won't tell anyone, not even him." He pats my back. "The doctors said they have never seen anyone recover so quickly."

I mentally repeat to myself that it was all worth it.

***

It turns out I do have a passport. I've never flown abroad, just to

104

Florida to see my grandparents. But Dad, Mona, and I drove to Vancouver a couple of times and to Whistler once. Instead of cards, we got full passports. "Just in case," Dad said. I guess this is the case.

I make a quick visit to Aunt Gemma. After I explain my plan to her, I ask her to give me some numbers and addresses in London. I also ask her to contact someone who can help me there.

My next stop is the ATM at the bank. I make a full withdrawal of the funds on my paltry college fund. But I can't use cash for the purchase I have in mind. Patricia meets with me, and I tell her I need her help. I try to give her the money.

"Absolutely not! I'll buy the ticket for you. You'll need money over there."

"Only if you let me pay you back when we're done with this mess," I offer.

"No, I—"

"It's non-negotiable."

I also ask her to fill a consent form for me to travel alone, if the airline asks. "I'm still a minor, after all. For a few months more."

Patricia says, "Huh… I don't have the documents. I'm not Patricia anymore, remember? I'm Jennifer now…"

It didn't occur to me that the reality of our situation might also have some practical consequences. "It's no big deal," I say quickly. "I'll ask Dad. Actually, I need another favor. Mona is safe. I'll be away. The only person unaccounted for is Dad. Will you take care of him? Hide him, or whatever you super spies do?"

After some reluctance, she nods.

"And did you explain to him about the witch stuff? Is he up to speed?" I ask.

"I did. Even with my Persuasion Charm, it wasn't easy."

I ponder that for a while. It was a shock to me when I found out about the covens. At least my father had a suspicion that *something* was not right with Patricia.

"Drake," she says, "you don't need to do any of this. I can do it. I've been *trained* to do it."

"Actually, I do need to do it. And I need to do it by myself."

She stares at me, putting her hand on my face. "You're so grown up."

"You wouldn't say that if you saw my room. Or the junk I eat."

She chuckles.

And I put my plan to work.

Chapter 16: Skye

I'm still caged in my room. I can tell the Sisters are in a hurry: my True Sight warns me every time someone arrives or leaves. And since Lady DeWees and Mum are in the manor all the time, my sense buzzes constantly. It's giving me a headache.

The day of my trial arrives. I don't even dread it anymore; I just want it to be over.

I take yet another long shower. Under the water, I take my time. When I soap my thigh, my silver phoenix tattoo glistens. I run my fingers over it. It brings back memories of Drake touching it, caressing my skin. I try to block the thought. Remembering him is not healthy for me.

While I dress in a long, formal black gown that was fetched from my house, I think of Mona. Mum, my only visitor, has kept me up to date. After the initial contact, Connor can't find Drake anymore. Drake's father is also missing, and Connor is desperate, thinking the Night covens captured the whole family, or at least one of them, to have some leverage against Mona.

I take my necklace in my hands. The pendant is a pentagram, like the one I gave to Mona, only mine is smaller, more delicate. I put it on and look in the dresser's mirror. With that, my clothes, my hair up in a prim do, and my Allure, I look way too pretty to go to my public condemnation.

Mum knocks on the door and opens it. "It's time," she says in a soft voice.

I must look shaken, though. She comes over and cradles my head between her hands. "Don't worry; you will not be alone. If they banish you, I'll follow you. I'll cut my ties with the covens."

I'm perplexed. "Absolutely not," I protest. "This is my mistake, Mum. I'll never let you do something like that."

She hugs me. "Whatever happens, I'm proud of you."

We'll be driven to a private castle owned by one of the Mothers. It's closed for public visitations, but it's been used for large reunions of Sisters for a while now.

My two guards flank us and we walk down the stairs and head to the cars.

We leave Waddesdon. I wish we were driving through London. Once, it was a magical place, for a magical me. In a few hours, both of us will be stripped from that glow, from that promise of a happy future. I doze off. A little more than an hour later, we're near the castle.

A collection of luxury cars awaits us in the parking area near the building. I recognize some Sisters, but they don't wave at me. They don't even acknowledge me. Mum is stone-faced, probably simmering from the lack of loyalty and sympathy from our Sisters.

We're guided to an enormous chamber. In the past, the wood-paneled room used to host meetings about politics, law, and civic discussions. Now, it is the last place I'll set foot as a member of a coven.

A discreet crew works as the people enter and take their seats. The crew hangs sacred symbols on the walls, banners with pentagrams, triquetras, and artwork. Some covens have their own symbols. A few incense burners are also placed on the podium and on the tables. Soon the large chamber starts to smell sublime.

The round arena-seating starts to fill up. Two entrances beneath the stands lead people in. The Sisters cluster in groups, more or less following coven lines. The witches presiding will stay at the bottom, behind a podium at the center.

I'm sensing the energy of each Sister in the room. I notice the tingling sensation increasing. Their signatures overwhelm me.

Since I can sense the direction too, my brain gets fuzzy with so much information. It's like having dozens of people talking to you at the same time, all of them demanding attention.

The tingling of a single Sister is like a faint energy wave traveling through my body. But all of them together make me feel like I'm in an electric chair.

My body starts to tremble. I try to control it, but with time, it only worsens. I'm shaking uncontrollably. "Mum…" I whisper.

"What, dear?"

I'm gasping for air. "The True Sight. Too many Sisters."

But I don't have time to go on. Everything goes dark.

***

When I realize I'm conscious again, I slowly stand up. My mother helps me.

"Easy," Mum says. "It's all right. You have only been out for a minute."

The electric buzz still crawls through my skin, but it's bearable now.

My mother looks at me. Her hands support my shoulders. "The Sisters have moved back on the stands. Does that help?"

I nod.

"Maybe we should postpone it," Elsa says.

Lady DeWees' voice is peremptory. "Absolutely not! We went to great lengths to gather everyone here today. I will not send them home because of something that may well be a deception."

My mother bolts upright. "Camilla, don't test me. Stop those veiled accusations."

They face each other like they might burst into fisticuffs at the slightest provocation.

"Very well," Lady DeWees hisses. "Let's start with the *real* accusations then."

We take our seats on table in front of the podium.

All the time, I fight the buzzing coursing through my body.

I look around for Judi. I haven't seen her since she visited me at DeWees Manor. I ask Mum about her.

"She'll be here," Mum says.

Lady DeWees, Elsa Dunivant, and one of the two older Sisters who observed my deposition preside over the meeting. They sit behind the podium, facing the audience. I wish Connor were here defending me, like he planned to do.

A ceremonial bell rings, catching everyone's attention. When the murmurs die down, Lady DeWees addresses the audience.

"Welcome, Sisters. I'm saddened by the reason that has brought us together here today, but I'm glad to see so many familiar faces. May the Goddess be with you."

Elsa and the other Sister—Helen Rothschild, Mum tells me—give their greetings.

"This meeting will also serve to update you on the latest developments of the Singularity search," Helen adds. She then

110

proceeds to read the statement I gave Elsa under the Truth Charm.

It's pretty accurate, including my reasons to hide Mona's identity.

"Skye, you haven't been to one of these proceedings before," Helen continues. "We don't use a formal prosecution or defense. We'll be the three judges today." She points to herself, Elsa, and Lady DeWees. "We open the floor to those who can contribute to the case and conduct all questioning. Your judgment will be passed by us—we don't have juries, but we take into account the opinions of the community. Do you understand?"

"I do, Ms. Rothschild. But Connor Wallace, who was supposed to speak for me, is not here. He has known me for years. I was expecting that he'd be heard in this matter." I have no idea what Connor was planning to say, but based on his demeanor, I thought he would be on my side. Without him, I only have Mum.

Elsa leans over to address me, but stops mid-movement. Her eyes catch something to my right, near one of the entrances.

A familiar voice coming from that direction echoes in the chamber. "That's all right. I'm used to replacing Connor."

I grip my mother's hand. My heart beats fast and almost overcomes the intense True Sight buzzing. Maybe I'm still blacking out, having visions.

Drake is coming in my direction, an easy smile on his lips and a newfound swagger in his step. Judi, my dear Judi, walks behind him, trying and failing to hide an amused smirk. I turn to Mum, but she's staring off in the distance, her lips pressed together.

He came for me.

Chapter 17: Drake

Holy craparoni. This is much harder than I expected. I was so confident on the plane, but this is sobering.

"Good morning to you all," I say in the most chipper voice I can muster. "I'm Drake Hunter. The Singularity is my sister."

They don't know me here. I thought I could use it to my advantage. Show up from out of nowhere, like the surprise witnesses in those procedural shows Dad always watches. Law & Order, please don't fail me now.

But it's a gigantic room full of witches, many of them Elders or whatever they called themselves. I trust my plan, but I can't help but feel intimidated by this assembly of serious people.

Judi could have prepared me better for what I'm about to face.

All eyes are trained on me, and the witches murmur amongst themselves. By now I know they can't curse me or something like that. Still, in the back of my mind, I expect a witch assassin will hit me with a poison dart any minute now.

Get it together, Drake. They're just people.

I'm not afraid of public speaking or anything; I've been doing show-and-tells since preschool, thank you very much. It's what's at stake that terrifies me: if I botch it, Skye will probably be kicked out.

To hell with that. I smile at everyone like I know what I'm doing.

Fake it till you make it, Drake. It's as simple as that.

"Who is this?" one of the witches in the judge's stand demands. At least, I'm guessing all of them are witches. "What's going on?"

Skye's mouth is open.

It seems all the Sisters in the chamber are talking at the same time. The woman is forced to use the bell again. Instead of addressing me, she focuses on Skye's mother. "Katherine?"

"Hm?" Katherine's fake aloofness doesn't fool anyone for a second.

"Care to explain?"

"Oh, certainly, Lady DeWees. This young man contacted me saying he would be visiting England and that he would love to take part in this... event. My dear friend Judi was kind enough to give him a ride here." She nods to Judi, who nods back. "As to your next question: he is an interested party, as he just mentioned."

I walk to Skye's table and stand by her side. I sneak a peek at her. She seems bewildered, staring at me like I'm an apparition.

"But this is not about him. It's about your daughter," the Lady answers. Is she a Lady, or a Dame, or what? I feel like I should have brushed up on British nobility etiquette.

"I believe those are inextricable," another judge says. "Skye, is this the young man we were discussing the other day?"

Wait, they were discussing me? This sounds promising.

Skye doesn't say anything, but her blushing answers for her.

"Of course. Young man, I'm Elsa Dunivant." Elsa turns to the other two judges. "I see no harm in letting him take part. He can give us great insight into Skye's motives. And I'm here, which guarantees his sincerity."

Lady DeWees is having none of it. She addresses me. "This is for

Sisters only, and you're a Knowing. You're also only a boy, and you actively conspired to break the Veil. Your words carry no weight here."

"I disagree," the third judge weighs in.

"Helen!" Lady DeWees protests.

"I believe he has valuable information," Helen says. "Drake, are you aware of the consequences of showing up here?"

I'm nervous as hell. I hope my voice holds. "I am," I say. "Judi explained them to me before I left the U.S."

"Well, I'm not!" Skye finally gets out some words. "What consequences?"

"They will arrest me—so to speak," I tell her, using the most relaxed tone I can muster.

Elsa says, "I wouldn't put it that way. But yes, you'll be staying with us until we ascertain the truth and this matter is behind us."

"Deal," I say.

"Sit down, please," the third judge says.

Judi comes over to the table. She squeezes Skye's hand softly and sits on the opposite side of me. Lady DeWees is still shaking her head. Helen calls another witch. I'm guessing she's the prosecutor.

I overhear Katherine whispering to Skye, "He's better looking than you let me know."

I can't suppress a grin.

"Good morning, Sisters. For those who don't know me, I'm Elizabeth Downing. I attended Miss Lexington-Ellis' deposition." She has a trained voice; maybe she's a real-life attorney. "We all know the facts by now. I'll just give them some context." She stares at Skye. Her disgusted gaze feels like a slap in the face. "The covens put their trust in Skye. Because of her unusual Charm, she was supposed to

114

find the Singularity. To bring her home. This was the most important mission anyone has been entrusted with in the last few decades."

Elizabeth circles our table as if she's a shark and Skye is her prey. "We all had faith in Dame Lexington-Ellis' daughter. We were rooting for this gifted young lady. We, with Connor Wallace representing us, planned everything so Skye would have the best chance to succeed in defending the covens. She would protect the Veil. Skye could have ensured that one of the biggest threats to the Veil in history would be contained. She was supposed to save us."

Her eyes look down. "But she chose herself. After identifying the Singularity, she decided that her schoolyard infatuation was more important than the safety of her Sisterhood. She knowingly deceived all Sisters. Skye lied, and she continued to lie to us as she befriended and trained the Singularity. To which purpose, one can only guess. Maybe she wanted to manipulate the poor little girl and use her powers for her own interests. Goddess knows she is selfish. She has proven that."

I want to punch that woman in the face, but I need to be smart.

Katherine, however, may do that for me. She jolts upright. "How dare you?"

Chapter 18: Skye

Of all the humiliations I have suffered in the last few months, this one stings the most. It's public, in front of my Sisterhood. And it's mostly true.

Elizabeth doesn't even acknowledge my mother's protest. "Skye could have gone into our history books as a heroine, a legend. But she will be remembered as a stain, a shameful example of someone putting her interests before her own coven and endangering the existence of all Sisters. She could have had our everlasting gratitude; now she'll have nothing. Not even our scorn, our pity. And not even our memories. She'll be banished from all the covens that pursue the light, and she'll be forgotten."

I feel small. I start to hate myself.

Lady DeWees nods along. Even Elsa and Helen are entranced by Elizabeth's argument. Heck, even *I* am agreeing with my accuser.

Wait a minute. Does Elizabeth have a Persuasion Charm? That's not fair!

"You make a compelling case, Elizabeth. Thank you," Elsa says. The mischief in her eye is gone. I thought Elsa was on my side.

I can't make out the whispers and comments from the audience, but they seem influenced by Elizabeth. This is not right. They told us there would be no prosecutors.

Before I can say something to Mum, Drake rises. "May I address the court?" he asks politely.

He looks good, in a navy sports jacket and black dress pants. His height and broad swimmer's shoulders make the jacket a great fit. Despite the gravity of the situation, I can't help but notice his cheekbones, his lips. Seriously, now, Skye?

He catches me staring at him and leans over. "Hey, you," he whispers.

"Hey, you," I whisper back.

"Don't worry. I've got this."

My eyes blink out of control, my chin quivers. "How?" I speak in low voice. "How can you?"

"Mr. Hunter?" Lady DeWees' voice sounds like nails on a chalkboard.

"I'm ready," he says, still looking at me. He shoots me a wink, and then faces the judges. "I'm ready, Your Honor."

Lady DeWees scoffs. "This is not a court of law."

"No? Please forgive me. It looks like one to me. Except, you know, no jury of your peers. No appeals. No witnesses who were there when the alleged misdeeds were done."

He looks up to the audience. "And that raises an interesting point, doesn't it? Ms. Downing's argument was eloquent. But of course she forgot to state one single fact, one single piece of evidence. As my best friend says, 'This is just, like, your opinion, man.' And of course, there are no witnesses here."

Drake turns to face the judging panel. "Isn't it curious? The only London representative who was in Seattle at the time is Connor. I've been told he expressly asked to be present at this trial. And yet, you rushed it, even though there was no reason to do so. But it's okay.

117

I've got your back. I was there when Skye found the Singularity. I can tell you exactly what happened." He looks at Elizabeth. "With, you know, *facts*."

Elsa takes advantage of his pause to say, "Luckily for you, I can tell facts from fiction."

"Excellent. Please feel free to interrupt me if anything I say is not true."

"Oh, I'm pretty sure everything you say will be the truth. Please keep that in mind."

Drake ponders Elsa's warning while pacing the space in front of the judge panel. "The day I met Skye, she saved my life. It wasn't the only time she did it, just the first one. Isn't it one of your most revered tenets, to cherish and protect lives? She didn't tell me she knew how to do magic. I put some pieces together, and she only admitted it to me when I threatened to go to the police. She was protecting the Veil. This is your most important belief, isn't it?"

Mum clutches my hand, but I don't turn to face her. My eyes are on him.

"I started to help her on her task, and she saved me once again. She entered a house where thugs and a Night Sister held me hostage. Skye confronted them all and took me to safety." He pauses to let that sink in. "Yet, here we are, putting on trial the only person in the room who actively did something to protect the Veil. Someone who risked her life many times. A trial! Witches trying witches? One of your own? I thought your kind had huge contempt for that. I thought the whole point of preserving the Veil was to avoid a new era of witch-hunting. So much for that, huh?"

Helen's eyes go wide with anger. "Mr. Drake, you're overstepping your boundaries."

He opens his arms. "Okay. This may not be a trial. In the end, it looks like you all have made up your minds. This is not a trial. It's a travesty, a sentencing hearing."

"Enough!"

Drake ignores the warning. "Skye once told me her life as a Sister was the only life that she knew. That it was *all* that she was. She couldn't bear to imagine a life stranded from her coven."

He points to the audience. His steely eyes burn with conviction. "Shame on you. This person, who's younger than you, by the way, acted on her beliefs—on *your* beliefs. And she acted with a conviction and bravery I doubt any one of you has ever displayed. She has been humiliated, tortured, and she almost died *three* times because of the mission you thrust upon her. She put her own fate on the line following exactly the tenets you all claim to follow from the comfort of your homes. Have you ever saved any lives? Have you ever been tortured in the name of your beliefs? Have you put your life repeatedly on the line? Now tell me who's selfish and who's selfless. Who, here in this place, really deserves shame?"

Tears streak down my face.

Drake points at me. "Not the girl I love," he says softly.

Chapter 19: Drake

Nailed it!

Chapter 20: Skye

He stares at me, a smile on his lips.

Everyone is silent while his words sink in. Even Lady DeWees takes her time before saying, "Thank you, Mr. Hunter. Please sit down."

Drake comes over and sits by my side, all the while maintaining eye contact with me.

I can't stop the flow of tears. My throat is closed up.

Mum speaks for me. "Thank you."

Still looking at me, he says, "Of course."

Lady DeWees rings the bell. "Now we will deliberate. Guards, please take Miss Lexington-Ellis and Mr. Hunter to the waiting room."

Upon hearing his name, I stand up. "Drake? You can't hold him!"

Elsa says, "We need to, Skye. He agreed to it."

I look at Drake, and he nods.

Mum holds my arm. "I'll be here. I'll speak on your behalf." Then she lets me go. I look around to see if Judi will speak up as well, but I can't find her anywhere.

The guards take us out of the chamber through one of the passages under the stands. Drake doesn't say a word.

We go to the second floor, to a large vaulted room with tall windows. The guards close the door and lock it. On the table, a tray with tea and biscuits waits for us. This tiny display of consideration feels weirdly out of place on this day.

I face Drake. "Thanks for coming."

"Well, I created this mess. I had to come for you."

I look down. "And thanks for defending me."

He is right in front of me. The proximity is unbearable. I want to hug him. I want his arms around me, comforting me, protecting me. I miss his scent, his warmth. And, oh, Goddess, I admit it: I miss his lips.

But I stay still. It takes all my inner strength not to kiss him. We can't have that now. No more mixed messages. I don't want to create something only to destroy it once again down the line.

His eyes analyze my face, as if reading all that I'm feeling. I think he knows what I want to do. But he doesn't take the initiative. Instead, he steps back and plops down in one of the antique armchairs. "Any good pubs around here?"

"What?"

"I've never been to England. I don't know the first thing. Will you be my tour guide?"

"What's wrong with you? We're prisoners!"

He looks at me, amused. "You know, it's a long flight here. Did you know it was only my second time in an airplane? I was a kid the first time, and I slept the whole flight. But I was totally wired for this one. Flying is unnerving. After the takeoff, I realized that I was hurtling at five hundred miles per hour over a vast expanse of water in a huge, heavy metal tube. Everything about flying is completely counterintuitive and illogical. To keep my mind away from that, I kept my brain busy. Thinking about you, about my life. About how all the women in my life suddenly are witches. You, Mona, my mother. My mother, the witch assassin."

"What?" I've always suspected his mother was a Sister, but an *assassin*? "How do you know?"

"She told me. We had an interesting conversation." He leans forward. "You know, she *did* stuff. Some amazing things, some dumb ones, but she had the guts to do them. Like Mona. And exactly like you. The witches in my life take control of their destinies, for better or worse. Now, I'm not a witch. But I can do things too. I'm not in Seattle, waiting for the result of your trial. I'm here, trying to make up for my blunders. To take you away from this nightmare."

"Yes, you are. Thanks."

"Don't thank me; I put you in this situation." He stands up. "Now, should we be going?"

"What?"

He finally touches me, taking my hand. "Skye, you saw how it went. This is not a fair trial. They stacked the deck against you. They decided on a verdict before it all started. I came here to defend you, but also to buy time if things went wrong. Judi is waiting for us in the car. She'll take us away."

I remove my hand. "No."

"Skye, you won't get another chance."

"No. I'll face it. This is my coven. I will accept their decision. I will not leave."

He stares at me with intensity. "No. You only run away from me."

Chapter 21: Drake

We don't speak for a long time. What's gotten into me? Another accusation on the day of her trial? Yet, I had that inside of me for a long time. She must know how I feel.

Over an hour passes until they call us. We're led to the main chamber again. Katherine is smiling. Yes!

"Skye Lexington-Ellis, please stand up," Helen says.

Skye does as told. She must have seen Katherine's upbeat demeanor; she must know things are looking up. Still, she's trembling.

"Ms. Lexington-Ellis, we have reached a decision—"

"A split decision," Lady DeWees corrects her.

Helen continues, "A split decision. We also consulted the Sisterhood, and most of our members agreed with the verdict. Your coven is happy to inform you that you'll remain a member of the Sisterhood. You'll receive an official warning for your failure to properly communicate your mission's progress."

Skye lets out a big sigh and looks up. "Thank you, Goddess!" Then she turns back and addresses the audience, "Thank you, Sisters."

Elsa says, "You should thank your Knowing friend for his eloquence and... devotion. We have determined that you acted according to the spirit of the Craft, albeit in a questionable way, to say the least."

"However," Helen adds, "You shall remain incommunicable until we resolve this Singularity situation."

Skye's smile vanishes. "But I—"

"It's all right, darling," Katherine says.

"Moreover, Mr. Hunter, you shall remain in custody as well," Helen says.

I saw that coming. "I appreciate the offer; I don't have a hotel booked. I was expecting to do some sightseeing, though."

Some witches in the audience chuckle.

"That's amusing, Mr. Hunter," Elsa says. "I have a few questions for you."

"Sure. I'll answer them to the best of my ability," I say.

"I'm sure you will," Elsa replies. "Do you know where your sister is?"

I remain impassive. "No, I do not."

"Would you tell us if you did?"

"Absolutely not," I answer firmly.

"What's your goal coming here today?" Lady DeWees pipes in.

I hesitate. "My main goal was to help Skye avoid being expelled from the covens."

"Your 'main goal'? But not the only one, then," Lady DeWees pounces. "You're clever with words. What's your secondary goal?"

There are so many answers to that question. Despite my control, I can't help but blush. Hey, I can use that.

"Mr. Hunter?"

"I wanted to see if Skye would consider… Please don't make me say it aloud."

125

One of the Sisters lets out an "Aww…" Despite the solemnity of the occasion, I almost smirk.

"Very well," Elsa says. "If we let you go, would you interfere with our search for your sister?"

A public interrogation by someone who is a walking polygraph should rattle anyone's nerves. But somehow the fake self-assurance I used on the trial has actually taken over me. I answer confidently, "Skye has convinced me that the best course of action is letting Mona stay under your protection."

I haven't answered the question again. I'm sure Elsa has picked up on that. She's letting me get away with it, though.

Lady DeWees is not so perceptive. "We appreciate that you're willing to help," she says. She has misread me. "However, given that you and Ms. Lexington-Ellis have interfered before, we simply cannot let either of you go at this moment."

I jump at the chance of ending the interrogation. "I disagree, but I understand."

"Very well. These proceedings are finished." She rings the bell. "Now we must move to other matters at hand."

They discuss who is going to chaperone us back to Lady DeWees' house, and Judi volunteers.

The Knowing guards enter the chamber and escort us to the entrance of the building.

Skye is not free yet, but she's still a Sister.

***

We get a luxury ride. Of course, it's not all fun: two guards ride with us, and the car doors are locked, but, hey, the leather seats are fancy. It's the prison bus for rich people.

At least the guards are not unsmiling, stuck-up cartoons. They keep an eye on us, but talk between themselves. They even joke to one another in a non-obnoxious way.

Skye and I are not that relaxed, though. The last few days were too much for her; she's exhausted and emotionally spent. She stares out the window. I'm not sure if she's trying to think up a solution, or if she's trying not to think about anything.

Either way, her silence suits me. I'm trying to calculate the best time to put my plan in action.

Even so, I sneak a peek at her. I'd love to be able to have her in my arms, to kiss her, to comfort her. But I'm not sure I'll ever be allowed to do so again. We haven't touched each other since I came here, and we haven't discussed where we stand, either.

I shake off the thought. I can get lost if I go down that road right now. My focus needs to be on my next steps.

I look back and see Judi's car following us. Skye's mother sent her to make sure we wouldn't be alone. Katherine is so smart—and such a good actress. She even made Lady DeWees feel magnanimous for letting Judi chaperone us to our temporary prison.

We stop in front of a large gate. A guard lets us in. Judi's car is waved in as well.

It's a castle! I feel like I'm arriving at Downton Abbey.

"Okay, I'm impressed," I say. One of the guards grins.

We all get out of the car and climb the steps leading to the massive front door. A large staircase with marble steps takes us to the landing on the second floor.

The grinning guard accompanies Skye to the door of a room. Before going in, she turns to me and says, "See you at lunch."

The guy locks her in and puts the key in his lapel pocket.

The other guard stands in front of another door. "Lady DeWees assigned this bedroom for you," he tells me. "May I see your backpack? After I inspect it, I will also need to pat you down for phones and other electronic devices."

"Sure," I say, shrugging. I zip the backpack open and reach for the small metal case. "Do you mind? It's almost time for my insulin shot."

"Go ahead," he says.

He starts to rummage my backpack while I open the metal case. Inside, I see the vials and the little injection. I quickly roll the vial of insulin back and forth in my hands. I remove its protective cover, insert the needle into it, and draw the liquid.

He then opens a bag of toiletries. "You didn't need to bring this stuff; the bathroom already has everything you need."

"Yeah, well, I wasn't planning on being a prisoner."

Still looking at the contents, he chuckles.

I stick the needle into his neck and press the plunger. He's a big guy, but the Sleep potion drops him almost immediately.

"Hey," the other guard shouts. He comes at me at full speed, his hands outstretched to grab me. I can barely take out the cologne bottle and spray him. I dodge him right on time.

But he's not knocked out yet. He grabs a funny-looking pistol from a holster inside his suit and aims it at me. His legs are wobbly when he takes the first shot. It zips past my head and hits the wall behind me, making the same whooshing sound Scythe's dart gun did.

I rush to my left, following the hallway. I hear two more whooshing sounds and a loud thud. The darts don't hit me. The second guard is on the floor.

Skye is banging on her door. "What's going on?"

"Hold on." I walk back and go straight for the key in the pocket of Skye's guard. I hurry to her bedroom's door and open it.

It takes her a second to realize what I did.

"Sleep potions, courtesy of Yara. And she even made them all three ounces or less, or they'd be in an airport trash can right now." My explanation needs to be brief. "We don't have much time. Where's your passport?"

"What are we doing?"

"We're going back to Seattle. We have some unfinished business there."

She shakes her head. "This is crazy." Her eyes scrutinize me. "Is this about us, Drake?"

I knew this part was going to be hard. "No. It's about Mona. And about you and your coven. Come back with me and finish what you've started. You can't help from here."

"But this…" She's moving in slow motion. The pressure of the last few days must be affecting her.

I grab her hands. "Skye, listen to me. We don't have much time. They will be knocked out for a while, but soon Lady DeWees will be back with a bunch of Sisters. This is our window."

She snaps out of her stupor. "Yeah. Okay."

"Good. Now, do you know where your passport is?"

"Lady DeWees took it. It must be in her room. I hope she didn't put it in a safe."

"Go get it; meet me at the front door."

I let Skye go, and she runs to one of the closed doors at the end of the hallway.

We hear Judi's voice coming from the first floor. "Is everything all right?"

I go to the handrail and see her in the center of the foyer. "Yes.

Thanks. We'll be ready in two minutes."

"I'll start the car." She goes outside.

I kneel down next to guards, search their pockets, and come up with two small phones. Those may come in handy. I put the phones in my pockets and all my stuff back into my backpack.

Yara designed a few potions and made them look as everyday items: toothpaste, over-the-counter drugs, and aftershave. Airport security didn't blink an eye. It actually freaked me out a little. If I can get away with it, I shudder to imagine what the bad guys can do.

"Got it," Skye says, holding her passport. "Got my money too."

We go into her bedroom and stuff a carry-on rolling bag with her clothes.

"Time's up. Judi is waiting for us."

We race down the steps and leave the house. Skye closes the door behind us.

"Where's the driver?" I ask Judi.

"After he dropped you off, he went back to pick up Lady DeWees and her guests. Sit in the back and lower your heads. A security guard is at the gate."

"I still have some Sleep potion left," I volunteer.

Judi gets the cologne bottle from me and leaves it on her lap. She motions to us to duck. The car parks at the gate.

"Already leaving?" the friendly security guard asks. We hear the hissing sound of the spray. His voice becomes slurry. "What's that? Who's in the back?"

I raise my head in time to see him leaning on the car and slowly sliding down to the ground like a puppet. I leave the car and push the green button on the security house dashboard. The gate opens. After the car drives through, I drag the sleeping guard until he's not visible from the sidewalk. I push the red button and rush out to the street before the gate closes.

"That should delay them," I say after I reenter the car. I sit in the front with Judi.

"Aren't they going to warn Heathrow?" Skye asks.

Judi smiles. "You are taking the Chunnel."

Chapter 22: Skye

Of all the ways I envisioned the day of my trial, none of them ended with Drake and me running away from my coven.

Judi drives us while I stare at Drake. He seems out of place in London. My hand has a mind of its own and touches his shoulder just to see if he's really here.

He turns back to me. "What?"

"Nothing," I say, feeling stupid.

Drake flashes me a grin and looks at Judi. "What's a Chunnel? I'm not current in witch-speak."

Judi chuckles. "It's the tunnel between England and France. The Sisters will be going to Heathrow straight away, but you're taking the Eurostar train to Paris. You'll fly home from there."

"Awesome. But won't a train take forever?"

"Not this one. Should be two, two and a half hours."

I butt in. "Then we arrive at Gare Du Nord and take another train to the airport. I've been there."

"Good," he says. "Because I have no idea what you're talking about."

His good-natured demeanor is startling. I catch myself tapping my foot nervously, but he stares out the window, oblivious, fascinated with the city.

"Young man, your phone is in the glove compartment," Judi says.

"Thanks for holding it for me." He finds the phone and stuffs it in his back pocket.

We arrive at St. Pancras station. While Drake gets our bags, Judi hands me a pair of plane tickets.

I glance at them. "The destination is wrong," I point out.

"No, it isn't."

"You think of everything!"

"It was his idea," Judi replies.

I get in the front seat and give her a tight hug. Her sweet, delightful perfume reminds me of my childhood. "I'll miss you."

"I'll miss you too, Skye. Now, go on. Clean up this mess and come home soon."

She stifles a tear, and I have to leave in a hurry so it doesn't trigger a similar reaction from me.

Drake approaches the window. "Judi, it was a pleasure. Thank you so much. But you still owe me a trip to the pub."

"Aren't you underage?"

"I'll only have a cranberry juice."

She smiles, waves to him, and takes off.

"This is awesome," he says to me. I follow his gaze. He walks over the side of the building and touches one of the red bricks. The gothic building must be a sight to behold for first-timers. He can't keep his eyes off the clock tower.

But I look around, concerned. I expect Sisters to come out from cars and the station at any moment, yelling "Aha!" My True Sight doesn't ring any alarms, but it doesn't mean they can't have Knowings following us.

"Let's go," I say. "We need to get our tickets."

"Use cash," he tells me. He hands over a few hundred euros.

I don't ask where he got it. I buy our tickets. Trains to Paris leave almost every hour. The next one is forty minutes away.

Drake is staring at the massive glass roof now. He takes out his phone and snaps a picture.

I drag him through the turnstile to the security area, and then all the way to the French Immigration Control line. My eyes search the crowd, expecting a Sister or a Knowing guard at any moment, but Drake is relaxed.

I still don't sense any witches nearby, but I tense up when the customs officer inspects our tickets and passports. She waves us through, though. Our bags are scanned and our passports stamped. Just like that.

We wait in the lounge until they announce our train is boarding. The escalator up to the platform gives me a bird's eye view of the area around us. No one seems to be following us or looking for us.

"We should get onboard," I say, still amazed that we haven't been detained. I point to the white and yellow train.

"Sure."

We sit side-by-side, facing a man with a laptop who definitely isn't interested in making small talk. Drake looks out the window.

I don't want to see people or movement. I stare at the carpet, its seemingly infinite diagonal stripes helping me relax. My body feels stiff, weak. I close my eyes and rest my head against the seat.

When the train starts to move, I barely feel it.

***

"Skye?" His soft voice awakens me.

I blink a few times, trying to orient myself. I feel his hands brushing my hair tenderly. My cheek is pressed onto his chest. I'm even clutching the lapel of his jacket like it's a security blanket.

"We're here. Paris."

I straighten myself up, embarrassed. I wipe a bit of drool from my chin, hoping he doesn't notice it. What's up with me using guys as pillows?

Drake seems amused by my confusion. He can't stop smiling. "The view was interesting. At first, it's just the boring tunnel, then I saw a little of the countryside. No strip malls, huh?"

We get our bags and leave the train.

"Now we take a train to Roissy. I mean, Charles De Gaulle airport."

But he isn't listening. Drake is back to his slack-jawed touristy stare, trying to absorb everything at once. "It's like the movies," he mumbles.

While he takes pics, I stare at the gigantic departure board. We have about three hours until our flight. The trip to the airport is about half an hour; it should be enough.

I turn back to Drake, expecting to have to drag him away from another European architectural marvel, but he's staring at me instead.

Chapter 23: Drake

Paris. I can't believe it.

It's a beautiful winter day. The sun comes through the roof of the train station.

An uncontrollable urge to sweep Skye off her feet and kiss her takes over me. It feels like all my life has been building up for this moment, when the girl of my dreams and I are alone in the City of Light, disconnected from the world.

But my brain butts in to remind me that, in fact, the timing couldn't be worse. She left me. We're only traveling together so we can fix the mistakes we've made.

Despite these rational thoughts, my subconscious still tries to sabotage me. "I wish we could be back here under different circumstances," I blurt out.

Skye blushes and looks down. She's about to say something.

I don't want to hear. I prefer not knowing than suffering a swift rejection. "Sorry. That's not fair. Forget I said it," I tell her before she can get a word out.

The illusion of the Euro-adventure disintegrates. Suddenly, the train station is not a magical place, but only concrete, metal, and glass thrown together. People are not mesmerizing characters in a French art movie; they become busy, hurried men and women with their own fears and schedules, leading lives as hopeless as mine.

She keeps her silence, looking at me as if I had just presented her with a calculus problem. This isn't fair to her. I should've kept my mouth shut.

"The train, you said?" I ask.

"Yes!" She sounds relieved. "We need to go to the airport. I've got the tickets."

"Let's go, then," I say.

She points to a detail on the glass ceiling, but I just nod. Everything has lost its novelty, its charm. I'm exhausted. Now that the adrenaline is gone, the jet lag is catching up to me. My legs feel heavy. My mind seems clouded too, which is great: I don't want to think about the awkward position I just put Skye in.

We take the train, but not as chatty, wide-eyed tourists. Now we look like everyone else: tired, haggard, and a little sleepy.

At the airport, we eat sandwiches in silence while we wait for the flight check-in. I look at the magazines at a newsstand, not really paying attention to them. My French is non-existent.

At the counter, the Lufthansa employee eyes us suspiciously. "Are you both minors?" She asks.

Skye smiles. "Only for a few more weeks."

"You're not eloping, right?"

"No. Definitely not," I say.

The woman looks at us, at our body language. We're apart, not touching, looking tired and bored. No way she thinks we're a couple. She nods and returns our passports to us.

"Nervous?" Skye asks while we wait to board.

"Why? Why would I be?"

"You said the flight to London made you jittery."

I did? Oh yeah. I told Skye I don't like flying. Was it this morning? Unbelievable. It feels like ages ago. "I'm so tired right now. Too tired to be scared."

She nods. Her lips are pressed into a hard line.

We board the plane. Our carry-on bags are the only luggage we're bringing with us, and I stash them in the overhead bin. Skye takes the window seat. I sit down next to her.

"Okay, if I fall asleep and lean on you, can I trust you to just take it as a sign that I don't have good boundaries?" Her tone is shy, almost as if she's talking to a stranger.

"Okay. And I wouldn't mind. I mean, in any circumstance." Damn, I need to learn to keep my mouth shut.

She immediately looks out of the window.

It strikes me as downright cruel: we're going to spend the next few hours so close to each other, but so distant at the same time. I'm dying to reach out to her, to touch her lips, to stroke her hair. I take a deep breath, but it only makes things worse: I inhale a whiff of her familiar perfume. It brings memories of much happier times.

Her profile against the light seeping in from outside brings me to the past. So many days and nights I dreamed of her gorgeous face: the graceful nose, the small chin, the inviting lips.

I'm not being fair. I came here for two reasons: saving her from the covens and helping me take Mona to safety. This joking or flirting or whatever is not part of my plan, and puts her in an uncomfortable position.

When the engines start, she turns to me. "Drake. Should we... talk?"

"We don't need to if you don't want to."

She uses a soft voice. "It would make things less awkward

138

between us."

"I'm sorry, Skye. I shouldn't have put you on the spot. I'm still in boyfriend-mode from habit; it's not like I'm angling for a reconciliation."

She opens her mouth, as if she's about to say something, but she thinks better of it. Her lips are locked again, and she looks down at her feet.

The plane is ascending, and the uneasy feeling in the pit of my stomach only grows.

Skye, still looking down, says to me. "I haven't thanked you for showing up at the trial. You saved me. No one could have been more eloquent than you. I still can't believe the Sisters were swayed by someone who's not a witch."

I embrace the change of subject. "It's all right."

She seems to unwind and turns to me. "How did you get there? Did Mum ask you to come?"

"No, no. I thought you might need help. No one in London knew all the details of what happened back home. I only asked Gemma to warn Judi of my arrival, because I had no idea where the witches hang out, you know?"

"What about the ticket? And the passport?"

I shrug. "I had the passport and some cash."

She narrows her eyes. "Last minute tickets are expensive."

"I had some money set aside in my college fund—"

"Drake! Did you use your college money? Why?" She doesn't notice, but she puts her hand over mine.

"It's okay. It wasn't much, really. It wouldn't make a difference if I decided to go to college."

Her eyes are wide. "I can't believe you did that. Mum can pay you back, you know?"

"Absolutely not. You know I would never accept it. Don't even bring that up."

She shakes her head. Is it really that shocking? I mean, that's what we do for our loved ones, right? I don't understand her reaction.

"Drake, that was an amazing gesture. You came all this way to help me... I'm speechless."

I don't know what to say either.

"I won't forget it," she says. Then she smiles the smile I've missed so much.

***

About an hour later, we have a quick layover in Frankfurt. I'm zooming by the countries I've always wanted to visit. I ask Skye about the places she's been, but later the conversation switches to her latest time in London with her coven.

She tells me a little about her last few days in London, about Lady DeWees and the other witches, about her deposition. She doesn't mention Connor, though, and I don't know if this is a good or a bad sign. Well, why would it be a sign at all? I'm not her boyfriend anymore; it shouldn't concern me.

Skye yawns and reclines her seat to prepare to sleep. I do the same. In a few minutes, she's breathing deeply. Her head slides to my shoulder, as she predicted. The scent of her hair fills my lungs, and I feel blessed.

When I drift off to sleep, I'm already dreaming of her.

Chapter 24: Skye

The noises on the plane wake me up. I yawn and stretch. Uh-oh, I slept on Drake's shoulder again. Maybe I should carry a teddy bear everywhere, just in case.

Thankfully, he's still asleep. I put a mint in my mouth, fluff up my hair, and stretch some more. Then I wake him up.

Drake blinks a few times. A glint of recognition escapes his eyes. He smiles and says, "Hey, gorge—" He catches himself, embarrassed. "Are we there yet?"

"Almost," I say. "Wow, ten hours. Did you sleep well?"

"I was knocked out. So tired. You?"

"The same. Why are we stopping in Vancouver?"

Drake brings his seat back up. He stretches, pulling his arms up until his hands touch the overhead compartment. "I thought the Sisters would be waiting for us at Sea-Tac. The closest airport is Vancouver, and we can drive home from there."

"That was smart. But we can't rent a car, can we?"

"Don't worry. Patricia will pick us up and drive us to Seattle."

"Who?"

He looks at me, surprised. "Patricia. My mother."

"Oh, yeah." It's hard to process everything. "How are you… interacting?"

"To be honest, I'm not sure how it's going. But she offered to help."

This is such a personal issue, I don't want to pry. On the other hand, her reappearance is not only his business. We have the coven angle to cover.

"Drake, I know this isn't my place, and I don't want to imply anything, but I must know if you have considered all the possibilities."

His expression becomes hard. "What do you mean?"

"Please don't take this the wrong way. You told me she was an assassin, right? This means she was—or is—a Night witch."

"You think she may be playing for the bad guys?"

This is hard! "For Mona's sake, we need to consider all the alternatives."

"No, it's okay. I'm not offended or anything. It's good that you brought it up. I thought about it, but I didn't have anyone to bounce ideas off. Her timing is suspicious, of course, but it makes sense too. She only showed up after Mona almost broke the Veil. I believe her, but she told me she has the Persuasion Charm, so all bets are off. And I know she's my mother because Dad says she is. But then, again, she might have the Shifting Charm you told me about." He scoffs. "It's maddening, really, when you start weighing what's true or what's not. And when you add magic to the equation—the possibilities are endless."

He definitely thought about it. "What do you think?" I ask.

"My gut and my brain tell me the same thing: she's being honest. I'm certain of that." He whispers, "Why would she tell me about being a murderer?"

"And do you believe she's doing what's best for you and Mona?"

His eyes grow sad. "I have to. I can't imagine anyone would abandon us—just to show up years later and destroy us—again. If there are such people in the world, I don't even want to live in it anymore." He looks at me. "We need to believe in the good in people."

My eyes water. I nod.

I forget everything about mixed messages. I pull him toward me and give him a tight hug. Whatever happens between us, I must keep him in my life. He's too rare.

***

This time, customs isn't a breeze. The official seems to be in a bad mood and asks us rudely, "Why didn't you go directly to Seattle? Why come to Vancouver?"

"It's cheaper," Drake answers simply. After that, the process becomes much less complicated.

He calls Patricia on a new phone. "She's already waiting for us," he tells me.

When I meet her, I'm a little surprised. When Drake told me that she was a witch assassin, for some reason I expected a badass warrior, a war veteran. The woman who climbs out of the car to greet me is shorter than I am, a curvy beauty with friendly eyes and a gentle voice. She shakes my hand with a limp grip.

Maybe that's her thing. Maybe she uses this sweet façade to sneak up on unsuspecting targets.

Ugh, Skye, way to dramatize things. If Drake is right, she left that life behind a long time ago.

I glance at the silver Focus. "I recognize the car."

"Goddess. Yes, sorry for the stalking." She seems embarrassed. "I didn't know who you were. I needed to make sure."

I choose the back seat. The three of us chat idly about the flight, the traffic, and the upcoming Canada-US border stop. I've been to Vancouver before, accompanying Mum on movie shoots. I like the city. It's not so different from Seattle, to tell the truth.

We clear customs without incident and take the I-5 to Seattle.

"Where are we staying, exactly?" I ask Drake. "By now, they must be watching your house and Aunt Gemma's."

He turns to face me. "It depends on how we're going to handle things. After you called me, I thought about it. Do you still believe Mona's best chance is to stay with the London Sisters?"

"I do," I reply. "The alternative is to be chased for the rest of her life by the Night covens."

"Believe me, that's not a pleasant way to live," Patricia chimes in.

I can only imagine what this little woman has gone through to stay under the Night coven's radar. "Right," I continue. "Connor made me assurances that my coven would do their best to make sure that Mona will lead a normal life."

My eyes flicker to Patricia, as if to check if she has an opinion, but she stays silent. Her lips are pursed, though.

"Okay, how would that work?" he asks.

"We should call Mona and Connor and arrange a meeting between them. We should be there too. Connor could take her to a safe place until they go to England."

"But why would she be safer in England?" Drake asks. "Don't they have Night covens there? What's to stop them from assembling a witch army and take Mona?"

I understand his doubt. "Oh, no. In England, we rule. Here in the U.S. and in continental Europe, the Night covens are strong. But back home, we fought our battles a long time ago. The Night witches perished or left. And many Sisters are in positions of power now. Mona would be safe there."

Drake nods. He's deep in thought. "Okay," he finally says. "I may need to talk Dad into it, but it's not like we have many options here." He turns to Patricia. "How's my father taking the news?"

Patricia shakes her head. "Not well."

"How did you convince him you're a witch?" He asks.

"I performed some spells with fire."

Drake looks at me. "Why didn't you show those to me? Those spells must be awesome."

"Come on, Drake, the Truth potion was wildly entertaining," I say.

Patricia grins and says. "My fire spells were too. Of course, Ben already thought that there was something odd with me to begin with, so convincing him wasn't that hard after all. Not to mention my Persuasion Charm. What did take a while was explaining Mona's powers and the whole situation to him. Now he fears he's going to lose her one way or another."

"He's right." Drake voice is throaty.

Poor Drake. I try to console him. "Think of it as Mona going to college early."

He scoffs. "But it's not the same thing, is it? First, it's not really her choice. We're all supposed to leave home to live our lives, to find our way, but Mona's life will be pre-determined, controlled. Mona will not be staying in a dorm or with a roommate in a tiny flat. She'll never go to a night club or to the beach by herself. She won't know anyone there and won't be making new friends."

I don't know what to say. I put my hand on his shoulder as he turns away from me and looks out his window.

Patricia grips the steering wheel with so much force that her knuckles turn white. Now I know from whom Drake gets this trait.

"I'm sorry, Drake," I say. "I wish there was any other way, but I just don't see it."

He takes a deep breath, curses, and says. "Let me call Mona."

"Does she have a phone?" I ask.

Still looking away, he answers, "No, Jane does. I don't know where they are, but I can call them on this burner phone."

Patricia and I exchange glances. We're both worried about Drake and Mona. In that moment of complicity, I start to feel I can trust Drake's mother.

He dials. "Yes, Jane? I need to talk to Mona." After a pause, he says. "Put her on speakerphone, then. I'll do the same. I'm here with Skye."

I point to Patricia. Drake waves me off. Patricia clenches her teeth.

"Hey, Drake." Mona doesn't sound tired or worried. That's a good sign.

"Hey, Mona? Are you okay?"

"I'm okay. Jane isn't torturing me or anything, if that's what you're asking."

Drake looks at me. "It isn't. But I'm glad to know you're okay."

"Mona. It's me, Skye."

"Hi! You're back. That's awesome!"

"Yeah," I say. I hope she doesn't mention anything about Drake and me. "Listen, Mona. The Night covens are closing in. We need you to come with me to England."

"No, Skye. I told Drake. I need to help Jason."

Drake gestures at me to keep talking. "You don't need to, Mona,

146

It's too risky. Is Jane forcing you to help?"

"Hey!" Jane says on the phone. "I asked her to, but it's up to her. It's your decision, kiddo."

Mona sounds confident. "I've made that decision a while ago. Guys, you don't understand. Jane's alone. If you take me away now, we're signing Jason's death sentence. It would be as bad as letting Boulder die. I can do something about it."

Am I being the bad guy here? I don't think so. I say, "But Mona, while you're hiding, the Night covens will keep killing Sisters. You may save Jason, but the time is ticking for the other witches."

"We need to get him quick then." Mona is unmoved.

"Mona, people are going to die!" I plead.

Mona's voice becomes even softer. "Help us rescue Jason then. I have this gift. I didn't ask for it, but I have it. I'll try to make the best use of it. I can't shy away. And you, Skye, you've got a rare gift too. With you, we can find Jason much faster. We can save him."

Drake looks at me, waiting for me to reply, but I'm speechless. Mona's words make too much sense for me.

Mona keeps pleading. "Skye, if it were Drake, you would do it, wouldn't you? You saved him before. I know you care. You put others ahead of yourself. You do it all the time. Do it one more time."

Maybe it's the jetlag, or the tiredness, but I have to make an effort so tears won't well up in my eyes.

"I'll do it," I whisper. "I'll help you."

"What?" Patricia asks.

Drake puts a hand on her arm. "It's okay, Patricia. Mona's right."

"Who's that?" Mona asks. "Is… *she* with you?"

Patricia feels the disdain in Mona's voice and winces, but she recovers quickly. "Yes, it's me." She slaps the steering wheel and faces Drake. "Do you all have a death wish? The Night covens are after Mona, and you want to take her to their doorstep?"

"It's Mona's decision. And Skye's," he says.

"Thanks, Skye." Jane's choked up. Wow.

"What now?" Drake asks.

Jane comes back to full badass mode. "I know where some of the Night Sisters are. I can stake them out with Skye. We can estimate the number of Sisters around and watch their patterns. Once we find out where they are keeping Jason, we'll figure out how to spring him out."

Patricia mumbles, "At least that's not a bad plan."

***

Jane and I arrange a meeting. I hang up and tell Drake that I need to talk to Connor.

"Why? We just escaped from your covens!" he protests.

"We need to tell him to stop searching for Mona and concentrate on keeping the other Sisters safe."

Drake points a finger at me. "No, Skye. Don't do it," he commands. "If Connor and your coven try to interfere now, they might tip off the bad guys. He's probably protecting the witches already, and he must have a plan to ship Mona out when the time comes. Too many people already know about this."

I'm surprised at his adamant behavior. And he may be right.

"Okay," I say. "But as soon as Jason is rescued, we're contacting Connor."

"Deal," Drake says, thawing a little.

I grin. "We only need to help the girl who tried to kill Mona and me. And then storm a Night coven's hideout."

Patricia turns to me, but says nothing.

Drake chuckles. "I still can't believe it. You came here to convince Mona, and she ended up convincing you. You're so lame."

"Hey," I protest. "She was right, what can I say? Give credit to your little sister, Drake. She's not just the Singularity, she's also a damn smart girl."

In the front seat, Patricia nods and keeps driving us back to Seattle.

Chapter 25: Drake

Skye is back. Not back with me, but at least back in Seattle. That's *something*.

What I told her in London is true: I have been thinking about my life a lot. I'm surprised at how I've been handling things. In a normal situation, breaking up with the girl you love would be devastating enough. And most people don't even have a sister who is super-powered, or a mother returning more than a decade after running away.

It's a miracle I'm still sane.

But in a sense I'm glad: at least I have a mother, a sister, and an ex-girlfriend to worry about. Those three witches are part of my life now—as is all the trouble that comes with them. I embrace it.

I just need to figure out how to keep them all safe.

"Patricia, where are you staying?" Skye asks.

Still with her eyes on the road, she replies, "We're all at a hotel near Eastgate."

I turn to the back seat. "Skye, can you stay with Aunt Gemma?"

"No, I don't think so. Connor said he wanted to have guards with all the witch families. But he might have included the Knowings too."

"Your house is out of the question too, Drake," Patricia says.

"They have people looking for you."

"What about Dad?"

"He's with me. Same hotel, different room," Patricia says. "Stay with us, Skye. It's safer."

I stare at Skye. I missed her face. Her mesmerizing blue eyes. The way her lips become thin when she's concerned. I wouldn't mind looking at her for the rest of my life.

"What?" she asks.

"Huh? Oh, nothing. I'm thinking." She almost caught me. I check my phone. Uh-oh. "Skye, I got a text from Priscilla. She sounds mad at me. And at you."

Skye lets out a grunt. "She must have been texting me like crazy. But I threw my phone away."

"She's at Boulder's. We should go there," I say.

Skye bites her lip. "I want to see Boulder. But I have no idea what to tell Pri."

"Tell her you had a family emergency. It's not technically a lie."

"It is a lie." She sighs. "Okay, let's do it."

I turn to Patricia. "Can you drive us there? Is it safe?"

"I guess, if no Sisters are around. If you don't think they have reason to monitor your friend's home, then punch the address into the GPS. But I thought you two were in a hurry."

Skye answers for the both of us. "We owe Boulder a visit."

***

Patricia drops us off and goes back to the hotel.

Serena answers the door. She frowns at Skye and me. "More friends, Drake?"

"Y-yes. How's Boulder doing?" I ask while she lets us in.

Still not smiling, she answers, "Better every day. His girlfriend is

151

in there."

"Girlfriend?" Skye whispers to me.

We knock on the door and go in.

Boulder has a big smile for us. Priscilla doesn't.

She is sitting by the bed, but as soon as we enter the room, she stands up, backpedals to the window, and crosses her arms.

The room is illuminated by bright lights. The tables are covered in get-well cards, pictures, and flower arrangements. It's not Boulder's style, but it softens the ominous presence of the remaining monitors, the hospital bed, and the IV drip.

"Hi, Pri," Skye greets her with a cautious voice.

"Hi." Pri's response is terse.

Skye hesitates but moves to the bed. "Hi, Boulder. Sorry I've been away. How are you doing?"

"Hey, Ms. Romeo. I'm better," he says. His voice is still throaty.

I'm so surprised at his recovery in such a short time that I don't correct his assumption. Skye is not Ms. Romeo anymore. Instead, I say, "Hey, big man. Looking good."

It's true. The color has returned to his face. He seems less emaciated. He's not the force of nature he once was, but he seems healthier and stronger than the last time I saw him.

"Thanks, D-Man. The doctors are amazed." He can't hide his pride.

How powerful can Mona be, really? Even when holding back her magic, she was able to not only wake Boulder, but make his recovery much faster than normal.

"Priscilla has helped me a lot," he adds, pointing to her.

He seems to be gaining control of his muscles: his arm doesn't waver when he raises it. His speech is much better too, even though he still talks in short sentences. I cannot imagine the effort it must be for him.

Priscilla breaks her silence. "He's been doing a lot of physical therapy and speech therapy—and asking for more. He's a champion." A smile starts to take form, but soon fades. "I've been texting you about his progress, Skye."

Skye's eyes flicker to me. "I'm sorry, Pri. I had to go back to London and lost my phone."

"Don't they have phones in England?"

"I've been running from one problem to the next, Pri. I didn't have time—"

"Oh, please. A two-minute call would kill you?"

I decide to intervene. "She was in a big jam, Pri. I had to go there to help."

Pri scoffs. "That's no excuse."

"Come on, girls," I say. "At least let's go to the living room. Boulder is not interested in this."

"Let them, D-Man." He grins. "This is better than TV."

Maybe the two of them have to work this out between themselves. I throw my hands in the air and sit in the chair previously occupied by Priscilla. Boulder and I look like the audience for a pocket theater play. Drama included.

Pri takes the initiative. "What happened? You disappeared the night Boulder woke up. Is your mother okay?"

Skye nods. "It was bad timing. They called me back to London. Mum is okay now."

They face each other, but Priscilla breaks eye contact and stares out of the window. "You're so frustrating," she says under her breath.

"What would you want me to do, Pri? I already said I'm sorry."

This ticks Priscilla off. She uncrosses her arms and walks to Skye. "Let's talk outside."

The two girls leave the room.

Boulder and I look at each other, and we both burst out laughing.

"Ouch," he says. "Stomach hurts."

"That was weird," I say. "But I'm glad you're okay, man."

"Yeah, yeah. Please don't kiss me. And I'm not okay. It'll be months of therapy. But, hey, I'm alive, right?"

He's a rock. He'll be okay.

"Hey, I missed Skye," he says. "Priscilla told me she visited every day at the hospital. Please tell your girlfriend thanks."

"She's not... We're not..."

Boulder frowns.

"We're taking a time out," I say. As if it were temporary.

"That sucks! Pri and I are... getting closer."

"Really?"

"Yeah. I mean, we're not going out." He points to the bed. "But that's good motivation for therapy. Huh?" He smirks. "What's up with the girls? I hope we're not missing a catfight."

And, with that, I know old Boulder is back.

Chapter 26: Skye

We enter the living room, but the nurse is there.

"Can we go out to the backyard?" Priscilla asks, pointing to the back of the house.

"Sure, honey," the nurse says.

I follow Pri outside and close the sliding door behind me. I've been here before. Boulder had thrown a barbecue party right after the school fire. We all had fun that day. But not today.

"I don't know what's going on with you!" Priscilla says.

I open my arms. "I explained it to you, Pri."

She grunts. "Ugh. Yes. You have explanations all the time. When you left the country the first time. When you made friends with the Weird Sisters. When I found the drugs in your purse. When—"

"It wasn't drugs!"

She ignores me. "When you were beaten up. When you left again and didn't answer my calls. It's a long list."

Pri seems to have run out of steam. She just stands there, facing me.

"What can I say? My life is a mess, Pri. A lot of things happened in a short time. I'm sorry, okay? I don't know how to deal with all this."

Her eyes become sad. "That's the thing, Skye. I'm your friend.

You should be sharing this stuff with me. You can vent to me, use me as a sounding board. Maybe I could even help you. But... I don't know. You're closed up. I don't know if you don't trust me—"

"I do!"

Her eyes tell me she doesn't believe me. She says, "And you never tell me *anything* is going on. I only learn it after the fact, after I press you for explanations. It's excuses and more excuses, Skye. Or maybe, lies on top of lies. Seriously, do you think this is what a friendship is supposed to be? How one-sided is *this* thing we have going on?" She points to me and back at herself.

It's as if her scolding has completely sapped me of all my strength. I sit down on the dormant winter grass. I feel deflated. "Some things I just can't share with you, Pri. Please accept that."

"That's the whole point, girl," she sounds tired. "Friends share. Even the difficult stuff. *Especially* the difficult stuff."

I shake my head.

"If I feel abandoned, imagine how Drake feels," she murmurs.

"What?"

She sighs. "He loves you. It's not only a crush. Even *you* know that, right?"

Her words sting more than she can imagine.

"He knows what the deal is. He forgives me," I say, but I sound way too defensive even to my ears.

"Of course he does. He's in love."

"He's not without fault, you know? You don't know the whole story."

"Of course I don't! You don't tell me anything!"

"This conversation is going in circles." Now I'm angry at her.

"It's because we keep coming back to the main problem! Don't blame him. Don't forget that you are the one running away, Skye. You did it twice already. When things got tough, you broke his heart. Twice. Are you going to run away again?"

I look at her. In her eyes, I'm a failure as a friend.

To Drake, a failure as a girlfriend.

To my coven, a failure as a Sister.

It all seems so unfair, but at the same time… they are not completely wrong. I may not be a failure, but I failed each of them.

All my defenses fall. Damn, Pri, you have a way of digging to my core.

I feel like crying—but I won't. I remember my mantra, when it all began: don't feel sorry for yourself.

Come on, Skye. You've been betrayed, humiliated, kidnapped, beaten up, knocked down, kicked, and left for dead. None of that broke you. It's not your own mistakes that will be your downfall.

We cannot be real friends with this lie between us. I've tried so hard to hide it from her. But if I don't tell her, she will never know my real essence. It would be like she never met the real me. That is not friendship.

I'm not afraid of the truth anymore. It's time to come clean.

"Priscilla, sit here with me. Do you want to see a nice trick?"

"What?"

I grin. "This will answer some questions. And maybe create many more. But you want me to share, right? You want the truth, no matter what?"

She looks at me, puzzled, and even a little scared. But she nods and sits in front of me.

I look at my fingernails. They are trimmed. Hers, on the other hand, are sharp and painted fuchsia. I grab her hand, stick one of her fingers out, and use her fingernail to make a deep scratch on my arm.

"Skye!" She pulls back her hand.

"Just look," I say calmly.

"Look at what? You made me scratch you!"

"Keep looking. Come on."

She stares at my arm, annoyed and pursing her lips.

"So?" she asks.

But then I see it. She sees it too. The width of the scratch has diminished. The thin layer of blood that had just started to come out stops growing. The change is almost imperceptible. If she weren't watching closely, she wouldn't notice it.

"What's going on?" All the anger has left her voice, replaced by curiosity.

"Keep looking..."

My Allure acts fast. The gash Jane made took over a week. But a scratch can be healed before the end of the day.

The blood starts to recede a little. The length of the white mark left around the scratch diminishes too.

It gives me an idea. I take out a small pen out of my pocket and trace the exact size of the scratch.

Pri gives me a brief inquisitive look. Her eyes return to my arm.

The tracing makes it easier to see: the wound is slowly but surely getting smaller. The skin that has been scratched, once white, becomes red, then pink, and then starts to blend with my natural skin color. The faint scratch mark is still there, but I know it'll be gone by evening.

The changes stop, at least to the naked eye. Priscilla asks. "What was that? How did you do it?"

"Remember when you picked me up at the park, when I was

beaten up? I stayed at your house. I recovered pretty quickly, didn't I?"

She nods. "Yeah, but you had your medicine. Homeopathy and whatnot."

I smile. "You thought it was drugs. It wasn't drugs or alternative medicine. I healed because those were potions. Magical potions. And my magic."

"Come on, Skye." She scoffs. "Is that your new age thing? Is that the 'truth'?" She makes air quotation marks. "That you're even more granola and believe in all that stuff?"

"I just showed you, Pri. Things don't heal that quick. Think of how I got better super fast that time."

"Still—"

"And now, think how *Boulder* was and what the doctors had said. Think about how he came back from the coma. How he's talking and joking with no signs of damage at all."

Her eyes go wide. She points at me. "You left the day he woke up," she whispers at me in a mix of awe and fear. "Was it you?"

"A friend of mine. But she used magic."

Priscilla stands up and starts pacing the yard. She can't stop rubbing her palms against the side of her legs, as if it can help her think.

I try to be sympathetic—after all, it's a hard concept to wrap one's head around—so I wait while watching her. She needs to process the information by herself. I'll just answer her questions.

And she has a few. "How... What does it have to do with... everything else?"

"It's a long story. And complicated. I came to Seattle to help my London coven find something. But those evil witches are around.

159

They threatened me and attacked me. My coven called me back to London."

She jumps and points at me. "The green light! When Boulder got better!"

I nod. "That was magic. That was the energy that helped him."

"I can't believe it. It's not possible."

I bite my lip. The Veil is broken anyway. "Well, there was the school fire. And the earthquake…"

Her brows draw closer. "It all started after you came here," she murmurs. "Skye, was all that… you?"

"No, no. It was magic. Out of control magic." I think that's enough for now. I rise and walk to her. I take her hands in mine. "Don't worry. It's too much, I know. I've seen that look before. At some point tonight, you'll doubt me and think there's another explanation for this. But it's all true. You wanted the truth, and that's the only one I can offer. I may hide stuff, but I don't want to lie to you."

Priscilla nods. At least she doesn't yank her hands from mine.

"Those are not excuses. I see now what you have been through. I get it. I admit I should've handled it better. I'm only trying to make you see I had reasons to do what I did and to tell those lies. Do you understand?"

"Kinda." Pri has the weirdest expression. She seems in deep thought and daydreaming at the same time. Like a focused haze of sorts.

"You must never tell anyone. Promise?" I ask.

"I'll never, ever, tell anyone," she says.

Chapter 27: Drake

The girls knock on the door and come in. Skye has a smug smile, while Priscilla looks like she's been hit by a bus.

I'm glad they came back. They took a long time outside. Boulder was beginning to show fatigue, yawning and becoming less focused on his speech and gestures. We had been watching TV for a while. He needs to rest.

"I think we should be going," Skye tells me.

While she says good-bye to Boulder, I stand close to Priscilla. "Are you okay?"

Pri looks at me as if she's seeing me for the first time. She grabs my arms and pulls me toward the door. "You knew about it, right?" she whispers to me. "About Skye's magic?"

With no idea of what transpired between them, I don't know what to reply. But Pri reads the answer plastered on my face. She punches me in the arm.

Boulder sees it. "Hey, don't break him. I don't have many friends."

"Is that so?" I say, pointing to all the flowers and cards taking over the room. "Define 'many.'"

"Thousands?" He grins.

***

Priscilla offers to drive us home in her Prius, but neither Skye nor I can go back to our homes. I tell her to drop us off at our hotel. She doesn't mention the witch thing again, and I don't ask.

When we get out of the car, Skye leans on the passenger window. "I'll get a new phone and call you."

"Okay," Pri says. "Take care." She drives away.

"The witch stuff really broke her," I say. "She looked like her favorite tanning salon had closed down."

"Don't be mean, Drake." She slaps my arm.

"Seriously. Maybe she thinks you're crazy. Why are you so sure she believed you?"

"You did."

"It was different." I shrug.

"Why?"

I almost tell her the truth: because I loved her. I was willing to believe anything she told me. Instead, I say, "You had healed my head wound, remember? In the woods."

She nods. "Yeah, right."

I mentally chalk up another awkward moment to my figurative bedpost. "Okay, let's talk to Dad and convince him to let his little girl leave him for the rest of his life."

Skye groans. "I wish we had another solution, Drake. I really do."

"Of course I know that, Skye. You risked everything to hide her. Don't ever think I don't appreciate it."

She stares at me.

"What?" I ask.

"Nothing. Let's find the hotel room."

***

My father is not convinced at all. Even with Patricia, Skye, and me

162

bombarding him with arguments, he makes a stand. "She's my daughter! She's a kid!"

He paces the hotel room, restless, as if caged. I think he wants to get out of here and punch the Night witches.

I feel a contentious vibe between Patricia and him, so I let Skye do most of the talking.

Skye says, "I can't possibly be in your shoes, Mr. Hunter—"

"Ben," he says.

"Ben, I'm not a parent. And of course you know Mona better than I do. But for the last few weeks, she and I got closer. We spent a lot of time together as I tried to train her in the Craft. She has her head—and her heart—in the right place. She grew up so much since I met her."

He scoffs.

"Dad," I say. "It was Mona who set up the house on fire that time. Her powers were out of control."

He looks at me in disbelief.

"Remember I showed you the fire magic?" Patricia says in a low voice.

His expression softens while he looks at me. "Yes. Oh, poor girl. And poor you. Mona didn't tell you, did she? You always felt guilty about it."

"She told me recently," I say. "And I understand why she did it. But do you see, Dad? She had to carry that guilt too, not to mention the whole secret about being a witch."

His foot taps the floor nervously. "It only makes it even crueler to take her from us."

"That's not the point I'm trying to make," I say.

Skye steps in. "She's much tougher than we give her credit for.

163

She had her life threatened, and she's on the run. But through all this, Mona remains clear-headed. Her powers healed Drake and the girl who attacked her. And Boulder too. Right now, she's risking everything to save a boy's life. She may be stronger than all of us."

He shakes his head. "She's just a teenager. I'm her only parent. It's my decision."

Patricia's eyes are downcast. She doesn't contradict him.

I stand up and walk closer to my father. "Skye's right. You and I look at Mona as if she still is that little ball of cuteness, that toddler with pigtails. But she's not a kid anymore. She hasn't been for a while, to tell you the truth. Mona is her own person now. It's out of your hands. And it's her decision, anyway, isn't it, Dad?"

We all look for words until Dad breaks the silence. "I need a moment alone. I'll go for a walk." He leaves the room in a hurry.

I ran after him. "Dad. Talk to her."

He stops and turns. "How?"

"I don't know where she is, but I know how to contact her." I grab the burner phone, dial Jane's number, and tell her my father needs to speak to Mona. "Talk to her," I tell him, handing him the phone. "I'll wait in the room."

When I'm back in the hotel room, both Patricia and Skye eye me with curiosity.

"He's talking to Mona," I announce. "It's in her hands now."

We spend about ten minutes in silence. Skye stares out of the window to the road below. Patricia reads something on her cell. I pace the room.

Dad comes back and hands me the phone. "You were right, Skye," he says. "Mona needs to be her own person. She will help the boy, and then you witch folks can take her and protect her."

164

Skye looks at me with a soft grin, but Patricia stands up. "What? Just like that?"

Dad looks at her, frowning. "Isn't that what you wanted?"

"It's the only solution I can see, yes. But you were opposed to it. What changed your mind?"

He shakes his head. "I can't specify a reason. Mona made some great points. It just feels like it's time for her to move on with her life. As strange as her life may become."

Patricia raises her hands in a helpless gesture. "I don't understand! You were so adamant."

Why is Patricia so worked up? Dad has agreed with our plan. I fear she will change his mind back. I step in. "It's settled then. Dad, we'll do everything to bring Mona to safety. Don't worry."

Patricia shoots me an enraged look, and in that moment I glimpse the fierce witch assassin she has once been.

"What can I do to help?" he asks.

I forget Patricia's misgivings. "You can't do much. We need the help of witches." I turn to Skye. "I'll talk to Yara."

Skye looks at me with a blank expression. "Oh, yeah?"

"Yeah. She knows about Mona, and she has been helping me."

"Okay." Skye turns back to look out of the window.

***

Jason's rescue is really going to happen. I call Yara and tell her I'm picking her up from school. We need to talk.

I don't want the students to see me. It's bad enough that Sean keeps texting me asking what's going on, and all I can do is send evasive texts back. Dad called the school and told them I'm absent because I've got a severe cold.

Instead of going to the school's parking lot, I wait for Yara on her walk home. I pull over next to a few houses down from hers. Soon I see her in my rearview mirror.

She notices me and climbs into the passenger's seat. She leans over and gives me a kiss on each cheek and a hug. "How are you, D? I've been worried. How did it go in London?"

"Exactly like I planned. Thanks for the potions. You're a lifesaver."

"And your damsel in distress?" She raises her eyebrows.

"She came back with me."

Yara yelps in delight.

"Hold on. We're not together."

"Yet," she says.

"We'll see about that. She's here to protect Mona from the Night covens. There's something else, too, and I need your help again."

I tell her about Jane and Jason and our agreement to hand Mona over when Jason is safe. I ask for more potions, especially Dispels for everybody involved in the operation.

"Do they know where he is?" She asks.

"No, but Jane has some clues. She has a list of possible places. She thinks she can narrow them down with Skye's True Sight."

Yara nods. "It makes sense."

A knock on the passenger window startles us. I turn, alarmed.

But it's only Greta. "Hey, guys," she says with a severe expression. "I stopped by to visit you, Yara."

I breathe a sigh a relief. I thought the Night covens had followed me.

Yara rolls down her window. "Hey, girlfriend? What's up?"

"What's up with you two? Sneaking out by yourselves? Drake, I thought you were sick."

"I'm… recovering," I say. No way am I telling her about Mona. Too many witches know about her already.

"Does Skye know you're hooking up?" Greta straightens and crosses her arms. "That's not cool."

"We're not—" Yara begins.

Greta interrupts. "Then why are you holding secret meetings? You've been disappearing a lot recently. Girlfriend."

Yara says, "We're just…"

But then Greta looks up, over the car. "May I help you?"

I turn to follow her gaze. A tall man stands before my side of the car. He yanks open my door and grabs me by the collar of my shirt.

But I'm a big dude too. I pull his arm back and punch him in the stomach, hard. He doubles over.

Out of the corner of my eye, I see Greta rushing over. "Let him go!" she yells at the guy.

A van comes to a sudden stop by the side of my car, behind the man. The side door slides open, and I'm face to face with Scythe.

She raises her dart gun, and this time she doesn't miss. A dart zooms past me, hitting Yara. The next one hits me in the neck.

Everything becomes blurry. The tall man recovers quickly and returns the punch to my stomach. It's now my turn to go down. I still see Greta trying to fight him, but the man punches her hard in the face. She collapses like a rag doll.

I'm barely aware of being dragged into the van. I hear the faint sound of Yara screaming my name.

Chapter 28: Skye

I plan a visit to Aunt Gemma. I need to know about the fallout from my escape. What are the London Mothers thinking? Have I sealed my fate? I only escaped after they acquitted me, but maybe they will reconsider their decision. I wouldn't blame them, really. I just wish they could see how I'm trying to make things right.

Drake's father is calling the school; he'll make up some lie to cover his son's many days of absence. I don't know what Patricia is doing. What does a retired witch assassin do, anyway?

Meanwhile, Drake will meet Yara to ask for her help. Why does it bother me so much? Drake and I are not together anymore, and I have no evidence that he fancies her even a little bit. Still, the lingering feeling does not go away.

The covens need to know what's going on. I need to talk to Connor, but I don't want to use any of the phones we have—I don't know who might be monitoring who anymore.

Patricia has lent me her silver Ford Focus for the day. I drive to a shopping mall and find a pay phone.

"Connor? It's me!"

"Skye! Are you all right? Where are you?"

"I'm in the U.S. Near Seattle."

His voice is enraged. "Goddess, Skye. Do you know what we've been going through? We thought you might be dead. Did you and your boyfriend run away, then? We knew you had knocked out the guards, but we had no way of knowing if the Night covens had gotten you or not. Your mother is close to a breakdown."

Mum! I thought she had expected all of this. I mean, she's the one who tipped off Drake with the help of Aunt Gemma. And Judi must have told her…

Oh, wait. She's an actress. She's been covering for me—and for her.

"Skye?"

I have to put on an act as well as my mother does. "I didn't know. I… Tell her I'm okay."

"How did you get here, anyway? After you fled, I had guards at Sea-Tac. No one reported a Sister arriving."

I grin to myself. Drake's plan worked. "I have my ways too, Connor."

"Is this a joke to you?" he growls. "Do you know where Mona is?"

"No."

He curses. "Skye. Listen to me. When I pulled some guards from the hospital, the Night covens jumped in. They took the girl in a coma."

"Brianna?"

"Yes, she's missing. The Seattle police are searching for her. Do you know what that means? They'll wake her up. She'll tell them about Mona!"

I almost drop the receiver. "No!"

"We need to get to her before they do. No more games or half-truths. I've tried to help you many times, Skye. You owe me. Where is she?"

"Connor, I don't know."

His voice becomes a low growl. "Damn it, Skye. Of course you and Drake know. You're risking her life and the Veil. Again!"

What do I do? I don't think this is going to change Mona's resolution. She wants to help Jane. She's hiding already. And I promised Jane. If we stop now, Jason is dead.

I bite my lip and hang up the receiver.

Chapter 29: Drake

I open my eyes, but the darkness persists. Something covers my vision. My hands instinctively try to move to my face, but they can't. I'm tied up.

An unbearable headache makes me wince. It feels like a thousand tons are pressing against my forehead. It throbs. It comes and goes, and the anticipation of the next round makes it even worse. I hope I wasn't hit on the head; my battered skull can't sustain much more damage.

I try to focus on my surroundings. It smells damp, like a place with no ventilation. I'm lying down, and the sharp cold I feel through my clothes tells me I'm on a concrete floor. I run my fingers over what's restraining my hands. It feels like plastic zip ties. I hear steps and ragged breathing next to me. And someone else sniffling, not far away.

The steps come closer. People are moving in my direction. Despite the torturing pain, I don't move.

"That's quite a collection you've got going here, Miranda." A woman's voice. Rough, bitter.

"Don't worry. We'll start cleaning house soon," another woman responds. Miranda, probably. Her voice has a high tone, and she speaks with a simmering rage.

"Is that why you brought me here? Who are they?"

"This young boy here is Jason. Remember the girl who could steal magical energy? Jane? This is her brother. She went rogue, and we were hoping she'd be back for him, but that was a waste of time."

"And this one?"

A sharp kick in my ribs makes me moan.

"Oh, he's awake," Miranda says.

My blindfold is ripped off. I squint to adjust my eyes to the lights. A small woman with red hair is kneeling by my side, staring at me. Miranda. "Look at you. If I had kept the princess, now I'd have a set."

"Princess?" the other woman asks. I turn my attention to her. She's tall. Her worn face says maybe sixty years old, and her dyed white hair makes her face look even older. But she has weirdly broad shoulders and large hands, and the veins on her neck pop out. She looks massively strong, like a bodybuilder.

"Skye. The one who had claimed she found the Singularity. She dates this one," Miranda says.

The other woman crosses her arms. "I still don't know why he's here."

Miranda stands up and points to the other side of the room. "That whimpering one in the corner is Brianna. The girl in the hospital who we thought was the Singularity."

"Yes, but now we know she was a decoy. The covens wanted us to think they already had the Singularity."

"No. That's the thing. The London Mothers really believed she was the one—until the green light event. When they realized their mistake, they relaxed the security at the hospital. That's when we pounced and got her."

172

I've got the migraine from hell, but my brain is working overtime. I need to find out what they know. At least they're so engrossed by their conversation that they don't pay attention to me.

Focus, Drake. Focus!

The white-haired woman motions to me. "If she's not who we're looking for, what's her value?"

Miranda grins. "She was at the school fire. She's not the Singularity, but she knows who is!"

For the first time, the woman in command displays a sign of satisfaction: the smallest of smirks. "And?"

"After we brought her here, we had to wake her from a coma. We performed a long commune ritual and gave her a cocktail of potions. She's awake now but not in very good shape."

"How long would it take to make her speak?"

Miranda sounds excited. "We don't need to wait. She was mumbling names, and she already gave us what we wanted. Apparently, a certain Mona is the Singularity."

Oh, no, please, no! I look across the room and see Brianna, weak and emaciated. She's having a seizure. She's lying down, shaking, trying to move her arms. Her eyes are open wide in a terrified expression.

"We know who the Singularity is?"

Miranda nods. "We know who she is, but we don't know where she is. Don't worry, Kendall." She points to me. "He's going to tell us. That's why we got him. The Singularity is his sister."

I'm still terrified, but now I feel a little better. They depend on my knowledge, but thanks to Jane's Forget potion, I really don't know where Mona is. They can't get anything out of me.

And now I know the bodybuilder's name: Kendall.

Brianna lets out a howling cry. She starts to convulse.

Kendall's eyes narrow. "Put the girl in the room upstairs. "

"Uh, this is the only sound-proof room. And the girl's bed needs to be disassembled to move it. I can do it, but it may take a while."

"Just do it. She's driving me crazy with her wailing. There's no one around to hear the shouts anyway."

"I'll tell Liam to move her," Miranda says.

The pain in my head is still strong, but not as sharp as before. I hope it's going away.

"And deal with this one!" the bodybuilder says. "What are you waiting for? Just give him a Truth potion and get it over with!" While she talks, she leans slightly over Miranda, who cowers. Their height and weight difference must terrify Miranda.

"We did! We used the Truth potion. He doesn't know."

What is she talking about? I don't remember doing that? Was I so out of it that I didn't notice? I'm like a toy to them.

"Did you check for Dispel potions?" Kendall asks.

"Dispel? No, why would we? They're so rare. He's not even a witch."

Kendall's voice rises. "But he's a Knowing, is he not? He knows witches, and he's the brother of the most powerful of all. How come it didn't cross your mind to check for Dispel?"

Miranda stammers. "We'll do it. We'll be thorough. But what if he doesn't know?"

Her boss stares at her with seething eyes. "I have other ways. If he knew and forgot because of a potion, we can find it. It'll scramble his head a bit. We probably won't get anything else from him. But that's the only information we need anyway."

Miranda nods. "I'm not sure I know enough—"

"I'll do it!" Kendall says.

I may get out of this alive, but my brain will be fried. I need to escape. Now.

***

Both women leave the basement. Now it's only us, the prisoners.

The pressure in my brain is subsiding.

I'm still on the floor, my hands tied up behind my back. The plastic ties go around a metal pole of some kind. Maybe it's a pipe. I try to shake it loose, first by bringing my hands around and pulling, and then by bashing my back against it. It holds and doesn't give up an inch.

My mouth is dry. No food or drink for me or my cellmates.

For the first time I take a look at Jason. He's been completely silent. He's a skinny boy, with shoulder length dark hair and the same angular nose shape as Jane. He's handcuffed to a metal ring bolted into the floor, but his hands are in front. He sits down against the wall, hugging his knees. His breath is ragged, and he stares at the opposite wall with saucer-sized pupils. His white shirt is stained, and his jeans are frayed at the hem. The toes of his bare feet are curled down, as if trying to claw the cold floor.

"Jason?" I whisper.

He doesn't acknowledge me.

"Hey, man. Look at me."

No reaction. I want to tell him that Jane's coming for him, but I don't want to risk it. They might be listening.

I turn my attention to Brianna.

She lies in an iron-framed bed. No linen or pillows to comfort her, only a bare white mattress. Her eyes seem to spin. From time to time, she has a small seizure, and her fists clench violently. She mumbles something, but I can't hear her from where I am.

I think of maybe talking to her, but I doubt she can hear me in her state. How can they let her suffer like this? She needs care; she needs monitoring. She was just forced out of a coma. No wonder she looks like she's in shock.

Yes, she tried to kill Mona. But no one deserves that. She went through enough already.

These two kids are broken. Even if they can get out of here, they will bear scars for the rest of their lives.

I hate those Night covens.

What can I do? I need to think.

The basement is a large rectangle with no windows and a single door. In the corner opposite mine, I see a metal pole. Next to the door, a bare wooden table and a chair. Next to it, a pile of cleaning supplies, tools, and oil cans thrown together.

My wrists and ankles are tied with the plastic strips, but Jason wears steel handcuffs. I can barely roll over, much less stand up. Jane's burner phone is gone, so I can't call anyone.

The phone. Do they have it? Who I called and who called me on that phone? Jane, of course. Patricia. Can they track Jane just by having her cell number? I don't know.

I need to escape before they get Mona's location out of my brain. How are they going to do it? That Hulk-witch seemed confident.

If I get away, I can bring the covens here and rescue Jason and Brianna.

But there are no sharp objects to use to cut my cuffs off. Maybe Jason could try to free me? The zip ties holding me are made of thick, strong plastic. I test them, putting my weight against the pole. The zip ties almost tear through my flesh. They cannot be broken or

176

untied with bare hands. I need a knife or a pair of scissors.

The door opens. A well-dressed guy around my age comes in, closing the door behind him with one hand while balancing a tray with witch utensils—mortar and pestle, candles, vials—in the other.

He comes closer and crouches six feet away from me, setting the tray on the floor.

"You're Skye's boyfriend, huh?" He smiles at me. "You're cute too. I could do either of you. Or both."

What? I decide to ignore his comment; there's not much space left in my brain for irrelevant information. Maybe I can make him talk.

"Do you know Skye?"

He chuckles. "Not as well as I'd like to, if you know what I mean."

Yes, I do know what you mean, bastard. Keep talking.

He goes on. "But yes, I do. I brought her here. Tough little thing. She can take a lot of punishment, you know? That's very… hot."

I struggle against my restraints. I want to pummel his smirking face into the ground.

"I'm Liam, by the way." He starts to take the contents from the tray and lay them on the floor. A cauldron, only larger than the one Skye had in her room. This one is the size of a punch bowl. Many candles. Several small containers with herbs. A collection of flasks I recognize: potion vials.

"What are they going to do to me?" I ask.

"I'm just a Knowing, like you, but I overheard them talking. They believe you did know where your sister is, or at least you may remember clues. Even if you forgot it because of a potion, they think it's still in there somewhere. Like, in your brain, but concealed.

They'll try to dig a little and see if they can uncover it. Of course, when you're searching a place for something, you may not leave it as orderly as you found it. You'll probably be damaged." He shakes his head. "Such a waste."

A little later, he and the tall guy who hit me take Brianna upstairs. Liam comes back and disassembles the bed. He doesn't talk to me.

Chapter 30: Skye

It's been over three hours since Drake left to meet Yara. What's going on? That's unusual, but it might be nothing. Maybe he just went to buy food.

I don't want to call and sound like a jealous ex-girlfriend.

In the end, the worry gets the best of me. I knock on Patricia's door and ask to borrow her phone. I call Drake.

But the voice answering is not his. It's Yara's. "Skye?"

"Yes?"

"Oh, Goddess, I've been trying to call you for hours. I called Drake's house too, but no one answers."

I steady myself on the edge of the table. "What happened? Where's Drake?"

"The Night covens took him, Skye. I'm sorry!"

My whole body becomes instantly cold. Get it together, Skye. You need a clear head. "Is he alive?"

"Yes," she says. "They just gave him a Sleep potion, I think."

"When? Where did that happen?"

"We were talking in his car when they showed up. Scythe and some other guys. They took Drake, shot me with a Sleep potion, and punched Greta in the face."

"Where are you now? Did the Night Sisters follow you?"

"No, they just wanted Drake. We're in the ER. I took his car and drove Greta here. She was looking pretty bad and going in and out of consciousness. And I have his two phones; they were in the car."

Why would they only take Drake, if they were after Sisters? They wouldn't take him unless... unless they knew about Mona.

Oh, no.

I summon all the calm I can muster. "Yara, I need those phones. I'll meet you at the ER."

She tells me the address and hangs up.

Now how do I tell Drake's parents that he's been kidnapped?

***

Patricia drives me to meet Yara. My True Sight makes sure there are only two Sisters anywhere near the hospital. That's Greta and Yara, and their signatures come from the ER.

I meet with Yara, and she hands me Drake's phones and keys. She looks at Patricia with suspicion.

"Who's the Sister?" Yara asks, wary.

"A friend," I tell her. "She's helping us."

"I want to help too," Yara says. "I mean it. Before they took Drake, he told me everything about Jason. I'll have all the Dispels and other potions you may need."

"Thanks, Yara. But it will get dangerous."

"I know. I don't care. Look what they did to Drake, to Greta!"

Poor Greta. "How's she?"

"She has a broken nose and a concussion. But she'll be okay."

I turn the cell on and look at the contacts. Only one number there. It can only be Jane's. I make the call.

"Drake!" Jane's voice is excited. Not giggly excited; more like going to war excited. "I was about to call you. We have a good lead.

180

We need you—"

"It's Skye," I tell her.

"Oh. Hi. Is he there? Put it on speaker."

"No, he's not here," I say. "That's the problem. He's disappeared."

Jane doesn't miss a beat. "And left this phone behind? He's been taken."

My knees weaken a little. Hearing her say it makes it even more real.

I hear Mona's voice over the phone. "What are you talking about?"

"You're on speaker, Skye," Jane says. "Tell us."

"He was going to see Yara. She's a Sister from Fremont—"

Jane cuts me off. "Yeah, I know her. What did she say? Is she sure it wasn't Connor's guards?"

"No. I don't think so. She saw Scythe. The witch assassin."

"It's the Night covens then," Jane says. "Sorry, kiddo." I know she's talking to Mona, but she might as well be telling it to me.

"They want to get to me," Mona says.

"Not if we get to them first," Jane replies. "Skye, no more hiding. Can you meet us? I found a house in Carnation, and I'm pretty sure it's the place where they're keeping Jason."

"They might have Drake there too," I offer.

Jane's voice becomes commanding. "Yes. We need you to use your True Sight. I need the numbers and location of every witch in the vicinity. Then we make our move."

"Okay."

"And Skye?"

"Yes?"

"Bring *our* witch assassin with you."

Chapter 31: Drake

I wake up to the sound of a door swinging open. It's the muscled woman, Kendall.

I'm surprised that I slept despite the stress. My brain is still fuzzy. I don't know if hours or minutes have passed. Maybe it's the blow to my head.

"Is that everything you need, Kendall?" Liam asks. Like Miranda, he seems scared pantless of her.

Kendall grunts. "I have a wicker chest in my car. Just grab it and bring it here."

When Liam leaves, she crouches beside me and whispers, "Are you sure you don't know where your little sister is? If you tell me now, I don't need to mess with your brain." Her breath is minty, but it revolts me anyway.

I don't reply.

Kendall shakes her head and reaches behind me. She grabs me by the zip ties and jerks my arms up. The movement stretches my shoulders back, but the pain is minimal compared to the one assaulting my head when I got here. I don't complain. I won't give her the satisfaction.

She raises her eyebrows and lets me go.

I sit on the floor again.

Liam comes back, carrying a large chest and showing a deeply disturbed expression. Miranda follows him. He puts the wicker chest on the table and takes a step back, as if afraid of its contents.

I hear someone whimpering, but it's not Brianna, who's upstairs, or Jason. It's coming from the chest.

Kendall walks over to the table and opens the chest. From inside, she brings out a puppy. It's a small pug with pitch-black snout and white and cream fur. The poor dog seems unusually subdued.

"Uh... What's with the dog?" Liam asks, running his hand through his hair.

"Miranda, where do you find your Knowings?" Kendall replies. "Don't they know anything?"

Miranda wrings her hands. "Liam, dear. We use animal blood for our potions. The more intelligent the animal, the more energy it contains."

"And the more powerful the magic," Kendall completes. She turns to me. "You see, boy? Whoever brewed your Forget potion is not a Night Sister and doesn't use all the available ingredients." She lifts the puppy by its neck.

If I remembered where Mona is, I'd probably tell Kendall right now. Maybe she would spare the pug. But I have no leverage here.

Liam shudders. "Can't you—I don't know—give it a Sleep potion?"

Kendall rolls her eyes. "Okay. At least I won't hear any whimpering." She shoots Liam a nasty look. "From any of you."

Liam doesn't care about the jab. He steps forward, taking a syringe and a vial from his jeans pockets. "I'll do it," he says.

"Maybe you're not as clueless as I thought," Kendall muses while holding the pup in a tight vise grip.

He injects the potion into the dog's neck. The puppy goes limp almost immediately.

Jason lets out a little yelp. Liam comes over and blindfolds him.

Kendall sits on the floor, facing me, behind the witch paraphernalia Liam brought earlier. She sets the sleeping dog at her side, picks up the herbs, and drops them into the mortar. She starts to grind the leaves with a pestle, her powerful arms bulging with the movement.

Miranda brings a small camping stove, puts it down next to Kendall, and lights up one of the burners. Liam pours water to boil in a cauldron.

I watch the preparations as if they are for someone else. I can't think of a way out of it.

When Kendall uses the fire to light the candles, I guess what comes next. She starts to chant in a low, raspy voice in a language I can't understand. She picks up the sleeping pug in one hand and a knife with a black blade on another. Without the slightest hesitation, she cuts and rips open the poor dog's neck. She lets its blood seep into the boiling water.

I twitch at the sight, and I feel like throwing up.

Liam rushes out of the basement. Kendall glances at him and shakes her head.

When she thinks she has enough blood, she drops the dog back on the ground. He just lies there, lifeless, like road kill.

Kendall scoops the ground herbs with her hands and rubs them together above the cauldron. She lets the herbs fall into the boiling mixture.

I don't know much about witchcraft, but the Goddess this woman is praying to can't be the same Goddess that Skye and the witches I know worship.

She turns off the stove. "We have a few minutes to let it cool until you have it."

I scowl at her.

"Huh. I don't think you will consider drinking it," Kendall says. "I'll get a syringe."

"No," I growl. "I don't want puppy blood mixed with mine. I'll drink it."

Kendal raises her eyebrows. "Really? I thought you'd fight it."

"I still have my dignity," I say.

Her smile is terrifying. "Not for long," she says, savoring the words.

***

When the concoction cools down, Kendall pours the contents of the cauldron into a white mug.

Since I'm still handcuffed with my hands behind my back, she crouches next to me and gives me the potion. She puts her oversized hand under my chin to make sure the liquid doesn't drip.

I take a tiny sip at first. It tastes like a mixture of water, blood, and herbs should: bitter and disgusting. My taste buds revolt, and my brain can't process the fact that I'm drinking puppy's blood. But there's no way out now. I man up and gulp down whatever Kendall offers me. Hopefully my stomach will reject all that, and I'll throw up.

"How long does it take?" Miranda asks.

"It should take effect soon, but we'll have to sift through his memories," Kendall says, standing up. She leaves the mug on the table. "The potion will jolt his brain, and all his repressed memories should surface. But we'll have to do some digging."

"What do you mean, repressed memories?" I ask.

Kendall grins. "It means whatever you forgot, via Forget potion or not. It should be interesting. You will spill your secrets, even the ones you don't remember."

I'm not sure what she means. "Like the Truth potion?"

"The Truth potion is kid's play next to this one, especially one brewed the Night witch's way with my magic." She sounds proud. "You're in for quite a trip."

While we all wait until they can dissect my brain, I try to think up a strategy. Should I tell myself to not give up Mona's location and reinforce that idea? Or should I stop thinking about Mona altogether, so it's not a memory easily recalled? I don't know the science or the magic involved.

The potion has reached my stomach. I can feel the weight, and it hurts a little.

But my head suffers the worst. The dull throbbing now spreads everywhere, even my sinuses and ears. A sharp pain pierces my skull, behind my eyes.

"Argh," I let out, despite my efforts to stay strong.

"It's starting," Kendall says.

She and Miranda approach and watch me with amusement.

Their curious faces are the last thing I see. I shut my eyes and press them together to ward off the pain. But it's no use.

A tsunami of images hits my brain. I try to cling to the real ones, like the basement I'm in, but the onslaught of visions make the real and the memories blend together.

I'm in a bed. I can feel the soft mattress and the warm blanket with Spiderman prints. A woman runs her hand through my hair. And the song. It's my mother's voice. She's singing.

I look at her. Patricia looks so young, so beautiful. Her hair is shorter, and her singing is a little garbled. She's crying. The singing stops.

"Go back to sleep, little D," she says in a shaky voice. "I will always have you in my heart. I'm sorry, but I need to leave to keep you safe. I hope one day you will understand. I'm leaving you because I love you. Take care of your sister for me."

It all goes black. I can hear a jumble of noises and voices. My eyes well with tears. It hurts, but it's a pain different from the ones attacking my head and my stomach.

I smell cigarette smoke. My coughs make my chest heave. It's hot, fiery. An inferno. My old house is on fire. Mona! Mona is upstairs. I dash madly to her room. Smoke is filling the whole house. She's lying still on the floor. Please, Mona, be alive. She's breathing! The drapes are on fire, and the flames spread to the bed linen and to the furniture. I scoop my little sister into my arms and leave the house, dodging the flares, fighting the fumes. My eyes burn and water, and I don't know if it's the smoke or the guilt. I carry her to the neighbor's front yard, leaving our smoldering house behind us. I lay her down on the grass.

"I'm sorry, Mona. I'm so, so sorry."

The heavy rain strikes my face. I lie in the mud. The new girl is kneeling down before me, her clothes wet, her hair disheveled. Skye. Her name's Skye. Even in the pouring rain, under dark clouds and the shade of the canopy, she looks radiant. She smears blood on my forehead while she chants and hums. My head hurts; my body is on fire. I feel like I'm levitating. Even with the searing pain, even with the elements attacking me, I feel comforted. But suddenly an immense sorrow takes over me. She's leaving. She's leaving me, and I can't stand the loss. It hurts so much.

My mind spins. I feel a buzz. Jane's warm breath and cherry lipstick tease me. I kiss her desperately. We land inside my car. She stops and asks me questions about witches, but I'm confused and can't help her. She's annoyed, but she softens her expression. She sits by my side and rests her head on my shoulder. We talk about losses, parents, and loneliness. Her hands entwine with mine, and she strokes my face with affection. "One day, I'll have someone like you," she whispers. Then she walks away.

They all walk away.

They are all witches. And they always leave me.

I leave them too. I leave my mother at Discovery Park. I leave Skye at the airport. I leave Mona with Jane at the Lake Stevens cabin.

They all wave at me. They're not together, but super-imposed, like a collage. Their faces are awash in sadness.

Then it hits me. They are not leaving me. These women are slipping through my fingers.

***

The first thing I feel is something cold on my face. I open my eyes. I'm on the floor, drooling. My whole body is sore, but the headache level is back to only a throbbing pain. It's actually an improvement. I try to twist, but my wrists are still tied up. I moan.

"He's back," Miranda says.

I see Kendall's knee-high boots approaching my face. She pulls me up, propping me against the wall. She uses a rag to clean my drool and my tears. She's smiling. Her genuine happiness disgusts me. "You did well, boy. It was very entertaining." She pokes the top of my head with her finger. "You had so much stored in there."

My throat is burning, but I say, "I didn't tell you anything. I don't remember talking." I sound raspy and bitter.

She chuckles. "You were talking non-stop! You walked us through all your visions. That's how the potion works. Otherwise, there would be no point."

My blood freezes. "Did I tell you where Mona is?"

"Yes." She pats my shoulder like we're buddies. "Thanks for that."

Before I can think, my hands move instinctively to strangle her. But they're still handcuffed behind my back. She notices my jerking motion and flashes an amused smile.

"Be thankful. You withstood a brutal potion. Your mind is intact. You're a fighter," she says. "It's a noble trait. We'll take care of it later."

"Are you going to kill me? I told you everything, it seems."

"No, no. We need to make your sister cooperate. If we torture you in front of her, she will do everything I need. It worked on Jane, and she's made of the sternest stuff I've ever seen."

I look at Jason, lying on the floor. He's just a boy.

Kendall's eyes follow mine. "Yeah, I know. Jane and Mona are two witches trying to protect their brothers. That's their weakness." Her smile turns devious. "Thank Goddess I'm an only child."

"Can you take his blindfold off?"

Kendall shrugs and removes the piece of cloth covering Jason's eyes. He doesn't move. He doesn't care.

Liam shows up at the door. "They're ready."

"Okay," Kendall tells him. "You and a few guards will watch him. Call Scythe and tell her to meet us at the place."

Then she turns to me. "Don't worry. You'll have your family reunion in a few hours."

Chapter 32: Skye

This is it. I'm terrified, but I keep a serene front for Mona's sake.

We're staking out the house Jane found. It has to be the place: I can sense several Sisters inside the house. We've seen constant movement throughout the day. Liam's Lexus and the van the Night covens used to kidnap me are parked up front.

Even though we can't tell for certain it's the place Drake and Jason are being held, it's our best bet by far.

When Jane goes back to her bike to get a snack bar, I ask Mona, "How was it? All these days with Jane?"

"They were... interesting," Mona replies. "I learned a lot."

"About what?"

She shrugs. "About Jane. About the Craft. And even about myself."

Jane's voice comes behind me, "And I learned a healing ritual. My first. One that Mona learned from you. Thanks to both of you, I guess."

Drake told me that Jane didn't have a Sister's upbringing, but this still surprises me. "This is like Craft 101. You didn't know any healing rituals?" I ask.

"I only knew hurting ones," Jane says.

I stare at Jane's scarred face. I did part of that. The vial of

Blinding potion I smashed on her face when she attacked me was directly my fault. The fire that burned half her face is her own doing, but she blames me anyway for not saving her.

What a long way we've come. Now Mona and I, two people she tried to murder at some point, are helping her.

"What?" Jane asks when she notices me staring.

"Stay down. We're freaking vulnerable here." I hiss at Jane.

She looks at me. "I can't find any other vantage point. Do *you* have any brilliant ideas?"

Mona pipes in, saving me from an awkward moment, "At least they can't hear us from the lodge."

The three of us are atop a hill, about three-hundred yards south of the Night witches' estate. Or "the lodge," as Mona calls it. It's a giant log cabin that reminds me of the one atop Mount Rainier.

I'm freaking out because it's just low vegetation from here to there. Anyone scanning the fields with binoculars could identify three human shapes lying low near the line of trees.

It's the perfect place to keep hostages. Carnation is a small rural city on the east of Seattle with many properties hidden from plain view. On the way here we passed a series of narrow, winding streets. The trees around us shield the lodge from the street, and the only access is the small dirt two-hundred-yard road that leads to the house's driveway. A creek follows the back line of the property. We can't even see the neighbor's houses.

"Can you still sense them from here?" Jane asks me in a friendlier tone.

"Only faint signatures. Five inside the house."

Mona taps her phone. She's been keeping track of the whereabouts of everyone in the house. "There should be Miranda, those two dudes in suits, the stocky woman, and Dragon Lady," she says, reading her list. Dragon Lady is the woman who always wears a tank top and has a silver dragon tattoo that covers all her upper back. We can see the tat from here. "Those are the Sisters. Besides them, we have the guy who took you—"

"Liam," I say.

"Liam," Mona echoes me, adding his name to the list, "and two more Knowings."

Jane curses. "Eight of them—"

"Eight that we know of," I remind them.

Jane nods. "Eight or more against four of us—I mean, if you can trust your friend, the witch assassin."

I'm tired of Jane calling her that. "Her name is Patricia. It's her son we're trying to get back, you know?"

"Where is she, anyway?"

"She's parked at the road exit. She can follow whoever leaves here."

Jane frowns. "We only have her car and my bike? When we get Jason and Drake, there will be six of us trying to make an escape. The more vehicles, the better. This way, we can split up."

"No, Yara is there too. She's driving Drake's car."

"Is that the girl who was with Drake when I got Mona?" Jane asks. "What's her deal, anyway?"

"She's good with potions," I say, in the understatement of the century.

We spend a few more minutes staring at the house. The wait is killing me.

"At least we have the element of surprise," Mona says. "We may be outnumbered, but we can take them."

"Well, kiddo, they might have the element of holding a knife to our brothers' throats. Then they would have all the leverage. We need to be smart about this." It's amazing how Jane's voice softens whenever she talks to Mona.

"I'm tired of waiting, Jane," Mona says.

"I've waited for months to get Jason back," Jane says. "This is the first time I have a real, tangible lead. Be patient. We need to do this right."

"But we can't wait forever!' Mona protests.

"She's right," I say. "We need to make the Night witches leave the lodge."

Jane slaps the ground. "How do you suppose we do that? Should we get a pest control van and uniforms so we can get inside? That only works in movies! Those witches are not dumb; if they sense something is strange, they will react. They might hurt the guys."

Mona sees something and reaches for the binoculars. "Skye, are they moving?"

I close my eyes. Their energy is hard to track from this distance. "Yes, four of them seem to be coming up and out."

"They're getting into the cars. All witches, but not Dragon Lady. And two Knowings."

"Let me see," I say.

Mona hands me the binoculars. I tell the girls what I see. "The suit guys are getting into the van they used to dump me in the park. Miranda and a Knowing take Liam's Lexus. The stocky woman and the other Knowing got in the white car. Liam is still inside, then."

"Why?" Jane asks. "Why would they leave at the same time?"

"Oh, no," Mona whispers. "They killed Drake, didn't they?" Her eyes water.

194

Jane grabs her hand. "No! Come on, Mona. They wouldn't leave the others. They won't kill the boys because they want to use them against us."

Mona takes a deep breath. "Okay."

"We need you, Mona," Jane says. "Whatever happens, don't freak out."

I return the binoculars to Mona. "Here, keep an eye on them until they reach the road." I grab my cell and call Patricia. "Three cars are leaving. Everybody but a Sister and a Knowing." I look at Jane, who nods at me. "It's time to move in. Meet us at the front gate."

Jane stands up. "Let's get our boys back."

Chapter 33: Drake

They will get Mona! I must do something.

I can hear the cars leaving. I guess the basement is not that soundproof then. But it means they don't care about the sound. We must be in an isolated house.

Think, Drake. I don't need to get to Mona; I only need to *warn* her. I know the Night witches don't have my phone, or they would try to call Jane, or track her phone, or do a reverse number lookup. But I called her enough times to remember the number. At least my torturers didn't try to get this out of me.

A phone is all I need, then. But my hands are tied to the pole. Maybe I can get the Liam guy here, head-butt him, and get his phone.

If the basement is not soundproof, Liam can hear us. I think about calling his name, but it would make him suspicious.

"Hey, Jason," I whisper.

He doesn't answer.

"Dude, I need your help!" I hiss.

He turns his head and looks at me. "What?" he asks in a hoarse voice.

"I'm going to get that guy here, and we're going to jump him to get his phone."

His eyes spark. "And call 911."

Good point. "Yes! Can you start yelling like crazy? When Liam comes and kneels down to see what's wrong with you, I can hit him from behind, and then you can kick him, head-butt him, or whatever. Just don't let him get away."

For the first time, I see some energy in the boy. He nods. "Let's kick his ass."

"That's the spirit. Now, can you yell like you're in pain?"

"It should be easy. I *am* in pain," he says.

"Use it."

He closes his eyes, and then he belts out the most horrifying cry I've ever heard. I think Jason has been holding it in for a while. It's a long, pained howl that actually makes my arm hair stand up.

"Good," I whisper. What else can I say to him?

But he doesn't stop. He curls up on the floor and keeps belting those cries until the door swings open.

"What the hell?" Liam growls from the door.

Jason keeps up the barrage of howls.

"What's going on?" Liam yells at me.

"I don't know!" I say.

But Liam doesn't move.

"Come on, man! Do something," I plead with Liam.

But we both are startled when we hear a loud noise over Jason's screams. Like a gunshot.

Even Jason stops for a minute. Liam looks up and hurries upstairs, leaving the door open.

"What…?"

Shouts come from upstairs. Male and female voices overlap. Another shot.

Liam comes back, his face pale. A cell phone is glued to his ear.

"Come back! They're here!" he shouts over the pandemonium. He listens to the answer and says, "Got it."

He puts the phone back in his pocket and rushes to a corner of the room. He makes a big effort to lift a blue plastic container from the pile of cleaning supplies and tools. Then he opens it. A strong smell of kerosene permeates the room. He makes the container tumble over, spilling a yellowish liquid on the floor.

"Liam, no!" I shout.

He scurries to the door and produces a cigarette lighter. He doesn't look at us before lighting it, throwing it on the ground, and rushing upstairs, not even bothering to close the door.

The liquid catches fire instantly. Jason and I immediately stand up.

I'm unable to talk, and I can't go anywhere. Jason is out of yells. He's just transfixed by the flickering flames.

I watch while the spillage rolls around the ground in random directions, teasing us with their trajectory. We are at the mercy of the whims of the murderous liquid.

The flames are high. But they're not the greatest threat to us. This room has no windows, and the only door, even open, is not enough to allow ventilation.

At least the fumes will knock us out before we burn.

Chapter 34: Skye

Jane and I ride on her bike. We're going downhill fast, the wind lashing at us. Mona stayed behind as a lookout. At least that's what we told her. The real reason is that we don't want her to be there if things go south. It would be terribly ironic that we ended up handing her over to the Night covens. She should be safe hidden up on the hill.

Patricia's car is coming from the road. Right behind her, Yara follows in Drake's Volvo.

The lodge is a large, sprawling one-story house. They have stables in the back. After many of the witches left, only one car, an Avalanche, is in the driveway. One more clue that they didn't leave many guards. I instinctively touch my jeans pocket. The vials are still there.

The bike hits a bump, making me almost lose my balance. My hands go back to holding Jane's waist. I try to wrap my head around what's going on.

The girl who tried to kill me is giving me a ride. We're about to break into a place full of Night Sisters.

The noise from the vehicles must have alerted them by now. I had asked Jane if we should turn off the engines and roll down the road, but she told me the field is so open, the Night witches would have seen us and heard us from afar. They are waiting for us.

The large wrought-iron gates were left open. Jane and I arrive first, and she turns the bike around, facing the gate. The cars do the same. We all jump out of our vehicles.

Jane and Patricia run to the front door's sides and lean against the wall as if they had rehearsed it. Yara and I duck behind the Volvo. I ready a Sleep potion vial. Jane told me about the potion-filled darts that Scythe used against Drake. I wish I had a dart gun with me.

Jane looks through the window and nods to Patricia. Patricia tries the front door, but it's locked. She gets a lock-picking set from her back pocket and starts to work on it. I'm not even mildly surprised at her talent.

Patricia gives Jane an okay signal before putting her tools away. The two of them enter the foyer.

They must know we're here, but there's no sign of life from the inside. This is way scary. "Stay here," I tell Yara.

"I want to help."

"We can't all go in. It may be an ambush."

She nods. I enter the house.

The inside is full of country furniture made of big pieces of wood. A couple of deer trophy mounts on the opposite wall greet me. The smell of lavender incense is almost out of sorts with the rustic room.

Patricia is looking into the kitchen, while Jane keeps watch so they aren't surprised from behind.

"The witch is on the other side of the house," I whisper to them. Dragon Lady is buying her time.

We hear a thud outside. I turn and look out of the door. A bald man is on the ground, unconscious. Yara is grabbing a gun from his hand.

I go to her. "Is he…?"

"He's sleeping. He came from the side of the house and tried to sneak up on you. Go on," she says, waving me in. "I've got your back."

"Thanks," I whisper. But it gives me pause. We didn't know about this Knowing; maybe there are others waiting for us.

That's not a dart gun. That was a real gun, with real bullets. They will kill us. And why not? We're breaking in.

I go back in and tell the news. "They have more guards than we anticipated. They're armed. With guns. The kind that kill people."

Jane is startled, but Patricia doesn't miss a beat. "Kitchen's clean. If Dragon Lady is in the back, I'm betting that's where we'll find the basement and the boys. They might even be holed up there."

"We need to do this quick," Jane says hurriedly. "They will alert everyone to come back."

"Yara has the gun," I tell Patricia. "Do you want it?"

She shakes her head. "No. I made a vow."

"Your son is in there," Jane reminds her.

Patricia shakes her head again.

"Fine!" Jane hisses.

Patricia takes the lead in a long hallway. She holds a vial in each hand. Jane and I follow her, in that order. I have my Sleep potion at the ready. Patricia nods at a door to our right. Jane moves to open it while Patricia and I stand guard.

Jane gasps audibly. Her hand covers her mouth. I sneak a peek inside.

The room is bare but for an iron bed with a thin mattress. In it, a familiar figure lies. Brianna. She's not moving. Her face is a pale blue.

Oh, Goddess.

Patricia barges into the room and touches the girl's neck. "Dead," Patricia says.

All the air is knocked out of my lungs. "It was me…" I whisper.

"We need to keep moving," Patricia says. She leaves the room, dragging me out by my arm.

"You don't understand. I—"

She cuts me off. "Deal with it later." Her voice has an icy quality that makes me shiver. "We're here for the boys."

Jane puts a hand on my shoulder. "She's right. Now, focus. Where's Dragon Lady?"

I take a deep breath. "She's moving back," I say, nodding to the door at the end of the hallway. "I think she may be outside."

"That's why Patricia and I can't sense her yet," Jane says.

"Or she us," I say. "Let's go. Yara has potions and a gun; she will take care of anyone coming."

The door at the end of the hallway swings open. Before we can move, a tall man shoots at us.

"Argh!" I hear Patricia's yell. Jane shoves me back to Brianna's room, getting both of us out of the way.

I can hear his steps coming. Jane jumps up and pulls me behind the bed.

The tall man appears at the door, his gun raised. "Come out!" he commands.

I cower, trying to make myself smaller behind the bed.

But the man blinks rapidly and kneels down on the floor. "What the hell?" he groans. He is losing consciousness, but before he blacks out, he raises the gun and fires a shot at us. It misses us by a lot, hitting the window to our left.

He then slumps to the floor and stays there. A small blade

protrudes from his back.

"Patricia!" I say when I get out of my stupor. I rush outside the room. Jane follows me.

She's on the floor, her eyes alert. "I got him," she says. Her shoulder is bleeding.

"How bad is it?" I ask, pointing to the wound.

"It hurts like hell," she growls. She's sweating. She doesn't look good.

"Can you go on?" Jane asks without looking at her. Jane's eyes are fixed on the door, a vial on her hand.

"Dragon Lady is coming from the other side!" I warn them. Yara, please stop her.

Patricia tries to stand up. "I'll take care of Dragon Lady," she says, resting on her knees. "Get them."

Jane and I obey her. I take the lead. When I look across the doorway, a liquid immediately splashes on my face. A little woman, hiding behind a table, has just doused me with a potion.

She's surprised that I'm still up. Thanks for the Dispel potion, Yara.

"My turn," I say. I pop the cap off the vial with Sleep potion and throw its contents at her. She still looks surprised when she collapses on the floor.

This looks like a media room of sorts. Three doors lead further into the house.

"This place never ends," Jane says from behind me. "What do you think? We already got three Knowings, and Dragon Lady is outside."

"That leaves Liam and any other Knowings we missed. What's that noise?" I ask. "Is that your bike?" A loud engine noise approaches the house.

"Not mine. Scythe's!" Jane's eyes go wide. "We don't have time."

We hear a door slamming and steps outside. I look out the window on the left side of the room. "Liam is running."

"What's that smell?" Jane asks.

I know, but I don't answer. Terror freezes my heart. I slam open the door on the left—the side of the house Liam ran from. There's another room. On the opposite side, stairs go down to a basement.

And dark smoke is coming from there.

Chapter 35: Drake

I'm not going to die here.

"What do we do?" Jason asks, his voice breaking.

"We get out of here. Stay low. Try to set yourself free."

"How?" he asks while kneeling down.

I use all my strength to try to get out of the plastic handcuffs, but they are too tight. They rip my flesh.

So be it.

"I'll try to slide my hands out. It'll hurt like hell. Do the same."

"Mine are steel!" he cries. "I can't. The keys are outside the door, on the wall. I can see them from here."

Not anymore. The flames are high, blocking the door.

Screw it. I need to free myself before I can do anything about this. I kneel and then put my feet under me, pressing against the pole. I extend my fingers and twist my hands, making them the smallest diameter possible. Then I push my legs against the pole while lunging forward and pulling my arms with all my might.

"Argh!" The hard plastic digs into my skin, into my flesh. But it gives a little. The blood flow is cut; my hands become cold. The cuffs are like sharp, plastic knives skinning me. But I can't stop. I push and push, sweating from the effort and from the heat.

I let out a scream rivaling Jason's when my left thumb dislocates.

I give it one last push. The ties slice off a piece of my right hand at the base of the thumb. It's raw and bleeds, but I'm free!

"Help me!" Jason says, coughing. "The water!" He nods to the water bottles the witches were giving us. "Throw them in the fire."

"No!" I reply. I don't have time to explain. I stand up and wobble to the door, but a wall of fire blocks our way out. The smoke is too thick.

I get a glimpse of the keys on the wall when the flames flicker. I can't get to them directly. Maybe I can squeeze my arm between the fire and the wall. With my body hugging the wall, I slowly extend my arm behind the inferno.

But the flames lick the wall, and my forearm burns. I recoil my arm by instinct before any further harm is done. I reach for one of the bottles and pour some water on my arm. Then I try again. The heat is almost unbearable, but my fingers stretch until I feel the keys hanging on a nail. I go for it and grab them, but the last effort sends my arm into the fire.

A primeval yell comes out of me, but I have the keys. My shirt's sleeve caught fire, and I quickly remove it and stomp on it, extinguishing it.

"Got it," I tell Jason. The pain in my arm is unimaginable, but I have to do this.

My burnt arm, my useless thumb, and my injured hand make it hard to unlock Jason's cuffs. The smoke causes my eyes to water. But I finally do it.

I look around for a blanket, but nothing in the room can help us. I grab my shirt off the floor and douse it with the remaining water in the bottles.

"Here, Jason! Wrap this around you, cover your head, and cross through the fire."

"What about you?" He's terrified. I may be only a couple of years older, but he looks like a kid to me.

"I'll figure something out. Go!"

"No!"

I grab him by his collar, cover him with the wet shirt, and set him in front of the door. "One, two, three!" I throw him through the fire.

He tumbles over across the threshold.

"I'm okay!" he yells from the other side. "I'll get water!"

"No!" I warn him. "They don't mix! It will only spread the kerosene and the fire!"

Not that it needs help. The fire is taking over the half of the room close to the door. I go to the other side and stay low.

That's it. I won't save Mona. I won't get Skye back. I won't be a swimmer or an engineer. I'll die here.

My brain tries to fight through the immense pain in my arm, but I'm out of ideas. I'm out of time.

I'm sweating profusely. Each breath is a tremendous effort, and I can only do it between coughing fits. My head feels heavy.

"Drake!" someone else barks from outside.

"Skye?" I shout back.

"Is there another way out?"

I have all kinds of emotions inside of me, but the survival instinct kicks in. "No! Can you find an extinguisher?" I fight a coughing fit.

"Jane is getting water from the kitchen," Skye yells back.

"Don't do it! Water will make the fire worse. Get a blanket or something, soak it with water, and throw it to me." I cough a lot. "But do it fast."

My breathing becomes more ragged. My lungs don't suck in air anymore. My head feels light all of a sudden. In the millisecond before I lose consciousness, I'm thankful for it.

I won't feel a thing.

Chapter 36: Skye

I push my worst thoughts out of my head. I get the blanket from Brianna's room, not looking at her corpse, ignoring the image of death.

Even in the chaos, I can sense two witches coming into the house. They're at the front, where Patricia is standing guard, screwed up as she is. We can't get to our cars.

I meet Jane in the hallway. She gets the blanket from me and shoves it into the large pan of water she brought from the kitchen. When it's completely dripping, we rush to the media room.

"Two witches are coming!" I tell her.

"I know. I'll defend the door to the outside."

"I'm going for Drake," I say, trying to get the blanket from her.

Jane stops in her tracks, looking ahead.

In the media room, the door to the outside is open.

At the doorstep, Mona stares at us. "I'll do it," she says.

"Mona! What are you doing? You're not safe here," I tell her.

She grabs the blanket. "Too late. You can't wrap two people in it." She rushes down the stairs, and Jane and I follow her.

Mona doesn't stop at the door. She goes into the fire, not even bothering to protect herself.

"He's here! On the floor!" she yells from inside.

That's it. Mona can't drag him through the fire, even wrapped in the blanket. He'll burn. Why didn't she think this through? Goddess help me. "I'm going in!"

"No! We're coming!"

Then Mona emerges from the fire, coming through in a quick sprint. She carries Drake in her arms. He's wrapped in the blanket. As soon as she crosses the doorframe, she stumbles, and I rush to help her and Drake.

"Oh, thank Goddess. He's alive!" I cry.

He's bleeding from burns and cuts, his bare chest scratched, his arm badly burnt. But he draws short breaths still.

"Take him away from the smoke," Jane says. "And keep an eye on that door." She climbs up the stairs ahead of us and disappears into the hallway.

Mona and I carry him upstairs and lay him down on the media's room couch.

I caress his face. He opens his eyes wide. Then he starts coughing. After a few agonizing moments, he takes a deep breath. His gaze focuses on Mona and me.

"You're safe," Mona tells him.

"Not yet," I say. My True Sight helps me locate our enemies. "Dragon Lady and Scythe are at the cars. We have no way out."

Jane comes back with Jason on her heels. She offers Drake water from a glass, and he takes little sips. She examines his arm. "This is not too bad," she says. "You can live with that. Believe me." Her burned face is all the argument we need.

Jason puts a hand on Drake's shoulder. "Thanks," Jason tells him. Drake is too weak to answer him.

"Here, drink this too," I tell Drake while handing him a potion.

"You too, Jason." I offer the boy a second vial. "It's Dispel. We have all taken one. It saved me."

"And Yara's Strength potion saved you," Mona tells Drake. "But it's already fading. At least I knocked out that guy when I sneaked in." She points outside the window.

Liam is unconscious on the ground near the stables.

"We need to go," Jane says. "Patricia is holding down the fort at the front door, but more Night witches are coming back to the house. Dragon Lady and Scythe are just stalling us. We're trapped. We have to go through them to get to our rides."

"Drake, can you walk?" I ask him.

He grits his teeth. "I can," he answers, unconvincingly. He reads the disbelief in my eyes. "I can," he insists. As if to prove his point, he gets up without a groan. "Let's go."

That's my steely guy.

I can't help it: I lean in and kiss him on the lips.

Drake looks at me startled, then the corner of his mouth turns up. "It was all worth it," he croaks.

We all walk to the living room. I go ahead and close the door to Brianna's room. Later, I'll make an anonymous call to 911 and tell Mona and Drake about her.

Patricia is hiding behind a large solid wood table that she turned sideways to use as a barricade. Jane and I crawl there while the others wait in the hallway. We're close enough so we can hear one another.

Mona says from behind us, "Wait. Now we all have Dispels. We can just walk out and throw potions at them."

"They have guns," I say. I look at Patricia's wound. Her shirt is dark red, but the bleeding seems to have stopped.

She follows my eyes. "I used a Healing potion. That Yara girl is

211

handy."

"Where is she?"

"Dragon Lady came for her and tried a Potion on her. It didn't work, of course, so she hit Yara. I could only watch, I was still bleeding then."

"Didn't Yara use the gun?" Jane asks.

"It's not that easy to shoot someone," Patricia says. "But I don't think Dragon Lady will have problems with that."

"Then why doesn't she shoot us?"

"She and the other," she points to Scythe, "have been talking on their phones. The Night witches are coming for us."

I whisper to Patricia, "The other is a witch assassin too. Her name is Scythe."

Patricia just nods at me.

"She has a dart gun with potions," I add. "But if she saw that the potion didn't work on Yara, she probably guessed we're all protected like that. She won't be wasting potions on us."

The Night Sisters are right there, a few yards from us, hiding behind their cars. We can see them, but it's too far to throw the potions with any precision.

We're stuck. Time is running out. I grab my phone and dial. Jane raises her eyebrows at me, but I raise my finger in a "wait" signal.

"Connor! I've got Mona. Drake and Jane and others are with us, but we're trapped. The Night witches are coming, and they have guns."

"I was waiting for your call," he says. "Where are you?"

I give him the address. I had told him we would be near Redmond, so he's close.

"We're bringing everyone," he says. "Don't worry."

But I do. My True Sight identifies more energy signatures. Magical users are closing in on us. "The Night Sisters are here," I announce, loud enough so Connor and my friends in the house can hear.

We all look outside. The cars that had left are back, rolling down the narrow road that leads to the house. The roar of the engines makes even Scythe and Dragon Lady look back to see what's going on.

Patricia jumps up and does a mad dash for the front door.

"Oh, no," Drake says in a weak voice.

Jane and I charge after her.

Dragon Lady is slow to turn back and is taken by surprise. Patricia, even wounded, arrives at her side just as she's pointing her gun. Patricia blocks her rival's arm, and a shot echoes in the fields.

Jane goes for Scythe and tackles her to the ground before the assassin can get to Patricia.

I go for the Volvo and find the key in the ignition. The engine turns over. Jason, even hobbled and weak, rushes in Jane's direction. Mona follows me, supporting part of Drake's weight.

I get out of the car and drag Yara into the backseat.

Meanwhile, I see that Scythe is thrashing on the ground. I know what that is. I used it on Jane's goon once, and now her enemy just had a taste of the same potion: Shivers.

Patricia punches Dragon Lady in the face, and when the Night Sister takes a step back, Patricia throws a potion at her. Dragon Lady soon falls to the ground and goes to sleep.

Mona helps Drake into the back seat and joins me in the front.

The Night witches' cars are now too close. Patricia leaves the gun, still clutched in Dragon Lady's hand, and rushes to her Ford Focus.

Jane and Jason climb onto Jane's bike.

Patricia takes off in front of us, and I follow her. The road is narrow. We don't need to stay on it, but driving in the irregular field would make for a bumpy ride. With Drake and Yara in their current conditions, I'm not willing to risk it. Besides, the Volvo is old and has a hard suspension; breaking an axle is a distinct possibility.

We are headed directly into the three cars. It's a game of chicken we can't win.

I glance to my left and see that Jane took her bike off-road. The Night Sisters are ignoring her. Of course, they're after the Singularity.

All the cars are still on a collision course, with Patricia's Focus taking the point.

"Is she going to hit them?" I ask Mona.

"I don't know," she replies. "I don't know her."

Drake's voice comes from the backseat. "I strapped Yara in. We have airbags, by the way."

Airbags wouldn't help much in a head-on collision at this speed. Besides, if they stop us, even if we survive, we still lose.

Their cars careen downhill with fierce resolution. Forty yards from us, as if they have rehearsed, they split up: the van stays on the road, while the white car goes left and the black Lexus goes right.

"What now?" I ask, panicking.

"Keep going," Drake says. "Trust her."

Patricia takes her Focus off-road too, to the right. She's now on a collision course with the Lexus. They're approaching fast, but before they are even close, the Lexus loses the game of chicken: the driver swerves further away from the road. Immediately, Patricia makes a hard turn back onto the road.

Mona screams.

214

Patricia catches the van on its side, in the back. The van wobbles and flips to the side, veering off and clearing half the width of the road for our car. It happens so fast, I almost can't react. I just go around the van with a quick, slight steer.

My whole body feels cold. I check the rearview mirror. Patricia's car is spinning, but coming to a halt. Half of its front is destroyed. Smoke is coming from under the hood. I can't see Patricia, but I still can sense her. She's alive. I hope she's okay.

The suit guys were in the van. Both the Lexus and the white car are slowing down and turning around. They are after us. And we're in the oldest, slowest car ever.

We reach the residential road outside the property, and I barely slow down to make the turn.

"Where are we?" Drake asks.

"Carnation," Mona says. "Skye, go back the way we came."

She's talking about the 202, the main road leading here. But getting there is not easy: this car was not made for narrow, sinuous roads. On both sides, the lines of tall, densely packed trees make me feel like we're driving inside a canyon.

I give my phone to Mona. "Here, re-dial and call Connor. Tell him where we are."

When he answers, she asks, "Where are you?"

"Fall City road, coming from Redmond. And you?" Connor says.

"Still on the side roads, but heading to where you are. They're on our tail," Mona says.

"Come to us; we'll block them," he answers.

"Connor," I say. "This car is slow; they'll catch up to us."

"Just keep going!" he says.

I glimpse the Lexus in my rearview mirror. They're gaining on us.

215

Each tight curve on the road is another opportunity for their cars with better everything to get closer.

The white car is right behind the Lexus. I'm distracted, and I almost hit a truck on the opposite side of the road.

"Watch out," Mona says. "I'll keep an eye on them for you."

But I can't stop checking the mirror. The Lexus is almost on top of us.

We arrive at Highway 202. I make a sharp right turn and enter the road without stopping. A car swerves to the other lane, loses control, and hits the guardrail.

The Night Sisters are catching up to us.

"Jane is behind them!" Mona says. "Jason is not with her."

"She must have left him," Drake says. "Is she helping us?"

Mona turns round in the seat. "She's side-by-side with the white car. She threw something at them!"

"Did they slow down?" I ask. It would be beautiful if she could hit the driver with a Sleep potion.

"No. Oh, they tried to bump her out of the lane."

I catch a glimpse of Jane's bike avoiding a crash with a car in the opposite lane. She takes the far shoulder to avoid being bumped again.

The Lexus hits us from behind.

Mona gasps.

A Mini is ahead of me, but an SUV is coming up in the other lane, leading a line of cars. The hell with it. I pass the Mini and swerve back to my lane just yards before colliding with the SUV. The horn rings in my ears.

I expected the Lexus to be stuck behind it, unable to get through because of the opposite lane's traffic, but they pass the Mini using the right shoulder. They are right behind us again.

The True Sight tells me another witch is close. I check the mirror, but can't make out the Sister. "Who else is there?" I ask Mona. "I sense another. Is it Patricia?"

Mona looks back. "It's Scythe! She's riding her bike on the shoulder. Fast."

Where's Connor? He should be coming the other way to meet us, but no one is ahead of us in either lane as far as I can see. I also cannot sense Sisters coming this way.

The Lexus with Miranda and the white car with the stocky woman are right behind us. Jane is on her bike on the left shoulder while Scythe follows us on the right.

The traffic in the opposite lane is gone. No way can I try to box in our pursuers now.

"Jane's making a move," Mona says. "She took off her helmet and smashed the white car's window!"

I look back. The white car tries to bump her again, but Jane is ready and dodges the move. Then she throws a potion at the driver.

The white car jerks left again, out of control, and this time it hits Jane's bike.

"No!" I shout.

The bike falls. Jane slides alongside the bike over the road asphalt. The white car is hit with full force from behind, spins, and comes to a full stop. The car that crashed into it also comes to a rest, blocking the traffic behind them.

I turn my focus back to the road ahead of me. "Is Jane okay?" I ask Mona.

"She seems hurt, but she's moving," Mona says.

The Lexus accelerates, but instead of bumping us from behind, it goes left. It gains on us, and then it hits our car from the side.

"Goddess!" I yell as I lose control. We spin, and everything becomes a blur: road, trees, cars.

Our Volvo turns the wrong way and crashes hard against the guardrail on my side.

Mona hits her head on the dashboard. Immediately, I feel a surge of energy around me. A wave of green light washes over us.

I see stars. My head throbs.

The engine of the Volvo turns off. I look up. All vehicles that were following us stop, their lights going off as if in perfect synchrony. Scythe's bike stops, throwing her to the ground.

"Are you all right?" Drake asks from the back seat.

Mona whispers, "No! Yes. My head hurts."

Miranda and the Knowing scramble from the Lexus and come at us.

I grab the phone that Mona had dropped on the floor on impact. "Connor?" But there's only silence. "The phone is dead." I forget about it and try to turn over our car's engine. "So is the car!"

"Out, now!" Drake shouts.

He leaves the car first. My door is jammed, stuck in the guardrail. I need to wait for Mona to leave so I can squeeze through the passenger's door.

Miranda and the Knowing both shoot at Drake.

Mona yelps.

But it's darts with potions. The Dispel counteracts some of it, but Drake, already weak, burned, and banged up by the impact, wobbles and falls to his knees.

"Mona, run!" I command her. "I'll get Drake."

I glimpse back, but don't see any cars coming to our rescue. I can

218

only make out a couple of people in the middle of the road.

In that split second, I see Scythe pulling a pistol and aiming at Drake.

"No!" Mona says. She jumps out in front of him just as Scythe squeezes the trigger.

I watch in horror as the bullet catches her in the chest.

Chapter 37: Drake

"Mona!"

She falls to the ground right at my feet. Her chest is a lake of red. I don't care if I get shot too; I kneel down to be with my sister.

Her eyes are open wide. She doesn't blink. Her chest heaves; her mouth is open, trying to capture air, precious air.

I put my hands over her wound, pressing down to stop the bleeding. I feel the warm, viscous blood.

I look around, seeking help. Skye is getting out of the car. She's pale, a ghost of the girl she used to be.

My surroundings are distorted. Everything I see is blurred, everything I hear is muffled. Out of the corner of my eye, I vaguely recognize Jane throwing potions at our enemies. At Mona's killer.

The only person in focus is Mona. She's dying. And I don't know what to do.

My eyes fixate on hers. "We'll fix you, Mona. Everything will be all right," I lie to her.

Skye yells, "Call 911!"

Jane says her phone is dead. They reach for Mona's cell, but it doesn't work either.

The road is strangely silent. No sounds of cars, no shouts. The only noise is Mona's gurgling. This is not happening.

"Jane," Mona says.

Jane kneels besides me. "I'm here, kiddo."

Mona coughs. "Remember… what I taught… you?"

Jane's sorrowful expression makes her more human than ever, even behind her grisly burned face. "I can't. I don't have the magic. No one has."

Mona coughs again, but this time blood spurts out. "I. do."

Jane's face becomes ashen, scars and all. She shakes her head.

My sister's torso jerks, as if she had an electric shock. Life is leaving her. "You. Promised," she croaks at Jane.

That's it. My little sisters is dying. "No, Mona. No," I whisper to her.

Her eyes come back to mine. "Let me go."

Then more blood comes out of her mouth, and her body stops moving altogether.

***

I stare at Mona in disbelief. It cannot end like this. It can't.

I feel Jane grabbing me by the shoulders. She turns me around gently, but I keep looking at Mona's lifeless face. "Look at me," Jane says.

Despite all my grief, I do what she says.

Jane takes a deep breath. "I need to do something. Now. Please don't stop me. Do you trust me?"

I nod. I have no idea what she's talking about. It doesn't matter anymore. Nothing matters.

Jane hands slip from my shoulders, down my arms, all the way to my bloodied hands. She lathers her hands with the blood.

I stare at her.

She gets a white knife from her back pocket and cuts her hand, mixing her blood with my sister's.

"Jane, how dare you?" Skye's voice is full of hatred.

"No," I tell Skye. "Let her."

A strange serenity washes over me. I see everything with a clarity I've never experienced before. I know what's going on. I don't know if it's going to work, but there's nothing to lose.

Skye's voice is high. "Drake, she's stealing Mona's—"

I look my girl in the eyes. "She's not stealing. And it's not Mona's anymore. Right?"

Jane kneels down and starts to chant.

I look around. Miranda, her Knowing, and Scythe are on the ground. Miranda's eyes move. Paralysis, I'm thinking. I hear steps on the pavement behind us.

"Skye!"

It's Connor and a girl I don't know. They're running toward us. More people are running behind them.

"They're our Sisters," Skye tells me.

"What's going on?" Connor asks when he's closer. He's almost out of breath. "Oh, no!" he says when he sees Mona.

The girl that came with him puts her hand over her mouth and lets out a little yelp.

Then Connor's eyes narrow. "Jane, stop right now!" He moves toward Jane, who's still chanting, oblivious to all of us.

I stand up and block his path. "No! She'll heal Mona," I tell him.

"What?" Skye asks.

"It's her only chance," I say.

Skye puts her hand on my shoulder. Her touch makes me even calmer. "Drake," she says. "I'm sorry, but it's over."

"It's not over," I say.

She whispers, "You can't come back from death, Drake."

Connor tries to go around me, "Jane is not healing anyone; she's using her Steal Charm."

I stop him, putting my hand on his chest. "Yes! To get the Singularity's energy. To bring Mona back."

They all look at me.

The girl breaks the stare-off. "I can't call 911!"

Skye whispers, "Goddess…"

I follow Skye's glare. Mona's body is letting out a faint green light. It climbs up in the air and floats towards Jane.

"Drake…" Connor says.

"If you try to stop Jane, I'll break the Veil. And my mother will. And my father will too."

This gives him pause, but he still doesn't budge. "I can't let Jane have the power."

I'm tired. My voice loses its edge. "Just have a little faith."

The flow of green light becomes steadier. It's now a darker green, and it doesn't float. Instead, it shoots straight into Jane's chest. Jane starts to smile. And something else changes on her face.

Her scars begin to fade. Her burned face starts to heal. The skin reconstructs itself as if filling the missing parts of her face with microscopic amounts of sand. Not only that: the lines of Jane's old face seem softer now, more beautiful.

The jet stream of green light becomes more and more intense, and the last of it hits Jane with a powerful blow. It knocks the wind out of her.

Jane opens her eyes. She has this manic smile. "It feels great," she whispers.

Connor says, "Jane—"

She raises a hand. "Shut up. It's not done yet." She kneels next to Mona again. I can barely look at my sister's body. "Now for the hard part."

Skye asks softly, "Do you need help for a commune?"

Jane shakes her head. "You couldn't possibly handle this much energy going through you. Not for what I'm about to do."

Still, Skye starts to murmur a quiet prayer next to me.

Jane's hands are still dripping blood, hers and Mona's, and she proceeds to draw symbols on my sister's hands, feet, and forehead. Jane lays her hands over Mona. The guttural chant of her Steal Charm is replaced by a gentle, peaceful humming. I've heard this before. In the woods, on the day I met Skye.

I try to look anywhere but at Mona. The Night witches are still on the ground, immobile. But Miranda's eyes are wide with awe. Even Connor and the girl with no name are slack-jawed. And quiet, for once.

But I can't stand to look away; my eyes return to Mona. My brain conjures the image of her in pigtails, just a preschooler asking where her mother was. I hope Patricia is okay.

Goddess of the witches, if you exist, please bring my little sister back. She once held your power, and she was a worthy girl. Now she needs your magic. Please.

Jane is covered in sweat. Her chant comes through gritted teeth; her brow is furrowed.

"Sisters," Skye whispers to me. Behind Connor and the girl, other people are arriving on foot. They look at Connor, puzzled, but he puts his index finger over his lips, demanding silence.

Little green sparks start to trickle down from Jane's fingertips over Mona's chest wound. It looks like a tiny green lightning storm.

It does nothing for a while, but then it starts to pool around the wound. Mona's torso starts to glow a little green.

The light becomes bright and alive. It moves and dances over Mona.

Her body raises and floats a couple of inches off the ground. It doesn't surprise me. It happened to me once.

Does it mean it's working? Please let it be so.

Jane keeps it up, chanting with a louder voice, determination stamped on her face. Her arms tremble; the veins on her forehead pop. Blood drips from her nose.

Skye has her hands over her face; just her eyes are uncovered. Her gaze is a combination of wonder and anxiety.

A loud gasp startles me.

It's the desperate sucking of air of a newborn. It's life entering a vessel. It's Mona.

She's back.

I crumple next to my sister. I cry tears of joy, relief, pain. Tears of everything. Her gasp brought me back to life too.

I cradle Mona's head gently between my hands. Her body heaves as she takes deeper and deeper breaths. She spits a little blood in between.

The green light is gone. Jane carefully inspects Mona's shirt where she had been shot. Jane wipes the blood away. Underneath it, the wound is gone.

"Mona," I whisper.

She opens her eyes. She blinks rapidly, as if getting used to a bright light after sleep. Her mouth curves up slightly.

Her gaze goes to Jane. "Thanks," she croaks weakly.

Jane looks like she just finished a marathon. She nods, still in shock.

"Yeah, what she said," I tell Jane. Despite my tears, I smile at her.

"Are we square now?" Jane asks.

I nod.

"Looking good," Mona says. Her voice is still raspy.

Jane looks confused. She touches her face where the burns were. Her eyes go big, her gaze wild. Despite her exhaustion, she jumps to her feet with catlike prowess, alert.

Connor raises his hand in a stop signal. "Jane."

"Stay away," she hisses.

"I can't," he says. "You've got her magic. You got her Allure. You're the Singularity now."

The witches alongside Connor are now watchful and lively. They spread around. It's seven of them, including Connor.

Jane starts to sidestep away from us, slowly. I don't know if she's leading them to an open field, or if she's just trying to protect Mona if something goes down.

Mona is breathing regularly now. Her face still looks grim, with the blood she coughed now drying and caking up, but I don't care. She's alive. Skye moves to her other side and adopts a crouching position, just in case.

"You know you have to come with us, Jane," Connor pleads with a controlled voice.

"I don't have to do anything!" Jane bursts. "I've been doing what you all want me to do since my Daybreak. Cillian, then Miranda, then you. You just want to use me. To cage me again."

Connor moves his raised hand to his side, signaling his witch friends to stay still. "Jane, listen to yourself. You're a danger."

"I'm not. I'm a trained Sister. I won't cause a disaster. I know

226

how to control the energy. I just did!" She points to Mona.

"It's not safe," Connor says, once again in a soothing tone. Is he using the Trust Charm?

"It's safe for *me*. Finally. Jason and I are free," Jane says. She takes a step back toward her downed bike. Her eyes never leave Connor.

Connor looks sorrowful. "I'm sorry. I can't let you go." His hand drops, and the witches pounce at once. Three of them rush to Jane, while the others throw potions at her.

Jane raises her hands in front of her. All seven of them are knocked backwards by an invisible force. The potions go through, but the Dispel takes care of them.

"How do you…?" Connor starts.

But two of the witches charge again. Jane does the same movement, just this time it looks more forceful. The two of them are knocked down on the ground.

Skye, Mona, and I are unaffected.

"Jane…" Skye says. But she's not pleading with her. "What was that?"

Jane stares at her hands, waving them in front of herself as if they are unfamiliar tools. "I don't know. But I can feel it. The energy. It's beyond anything I've ever imagined."

Mona's head is resting on my arms. "Enjoy my gift," she says softly.

Jane gives my sister a loving smile. "Enjoy mine."

Then her steely face comes back. "I'll make a deal, Connor."

Connor and his coven stand up, but they don't dare attack her this time. "A deal?" he asks.

"Yes. I'm going to leave now. I'll pick Jason up, and we'll disappear. I promise I'll never break the Veil as long as we both are safe. I also can control the energy, so I can pretty much guarantee no earthquakes or fires." She looks back at Miranda, who is regaining the use of her limbs and is on all fours trying to get up. "But if anyone comes after me, if anyone follows us, if anyone even hints at a threat, I'll unleash the full power of the Singularity over you. That will beak the Veil once and for all. And I'll kill you." She points to Connor. "This goes for you." Then she points at Miranda. "And *especially* for you."

"I can't answer for the Mothers," Connor says.

"Of course you can!" Jane shouts. "Don't play games with me."

"Okay, okay," Connor says. "But it goes both ways. If you break the Veil, it leaves us no choice but to come for you."

"Fair enough," Jane says.

Then she walks backwards to her motorcycle, keeping an eye on the witches. With a grunt, she brings the bike back up.

She doesn't even glance at Skye, Mona, or me. Jane climbs on her motorcycle and leaves all of us behind.

Chapter 38: Skye

Mona doesn't have Allure anymore, but she seems radiant nevertheless. Being brought back to life will do that to you. She can't stop smiling, really.

We just came back from the hospital. Patricia is there, being treated for multiple broken bones, but she's fine. None of the injuries are life-threatening. Drake's father insisted on staying over.

Now we're back in Mona's room. It feels familiar and safe. Like a sanctuary. I point to the candles and incense on her desk. "Still a Wiccan?" I ask.

"Yep. I may not have the magic in me anymore, but I have the faith," she says. "I wish I still were a witch; I was looking forward to one of those silver tattoos."

I'm glad that she's taking it so well. I'm curious about her near-death experience—or was it a back-to-life one? In any case, it's not my place to ask. One day I'd like to know, though.

Drake knocks on the door and comes in. "Total loss," he says. "My trusted Volvo is gone. Dad will receive a check with very few zeroes on it."

Getting off that road and back home was a nightmare. "What really happened with all the cars?"

Drake sits down next to me. "Mona caused a small EMP, an

electromagnetic pulse. It's a burst of electromagnetic energy that causes electronics to malfunction. That's why all the cars and phones stopped working. I kind of guessed at the time. When we left and I saw all cars suddenly stop for a mile each way, I was pretty sure. We studied that in physics this year."

"Drake, the engineer," Mona mocks.

"Hey, don't knock my science cred. And *you* were the one releasing all kinds of energy until very recently."

Connor had to send a couple of Sisters out of the blast zone just to call for help. Then he had to clean up the mess we made. Even though the other drivers and passengers couldn't film our magical spectacle on their phones, they saw what happened. Forget potions flew freely. And they had to clean up the road—all the cars and trucks. A few people got hurt, but none too seriously. Thank Goddess.

Except for one. I put my head down.

"What?" Drake asks, lifting my chin. "What's going on?"

"Brianna," I confess.

He comes over and wraps me in his arms. "Skye, you can't beat yourself up because of her. The Night covens brought her back from a coma using magic. You had told me it was risky," he says.

"And who put her there?" I ask.

"Not you!" He tips my chin so I face him. "You saved her, remember? When she tried to kill Mona, you rescued her from the fire *and* you healed her enough so she would survive. She only had a chance to survive because of you."

"Still—"

He cuts me off. "Promise you won't blame yourself."

I nod, but it's mostly so he'll let it go. My thoughts are swirling in my head.

"Huh," Mona says, snapping me out of my absent-mindedness.

"What?" Drake asks.

"It's funny. When you and I used the Singularity's power to save Boulder's life, Skye made a big deal about it. She said horrible things and left you. But Skye forgot one thing."

Mona pauses.

My impatience gets the best of me. "Go on!"

"Skye, you asked me to do the same thing for Brianna. And Brianna wasn't even our friend like Boulder. She had just tried to kill me, actually."

My stomach drops. Mona's right. How have I never seen that?

"And worse," Mona continues, "I had absolutely no training to control my energy then. I hadn't been trained, right, Skye?"

I've been blaming Drake for exactly the same thing I had done myself before.

"All right, all right," I say, raising my hands in a surrender gesture.

Drake turns to me. He seems as stunned as I am, but he quips in a mocking voice, "Yes, Skye. What's up with that? How are things up there on your high horse?"

"I-I—" I stammer.

"I'll help you out," he says. "Repeat after me. I. Forgive. You."

"I forgive you," I say, but using my grumpy voice.

"Now? You could've saved me a ticket to London!"

"Yeah, you used your college money to go to London and defend me. A lot of money, Drake." I blush as soon as I say it.

He shrugs. "There wasn't much there anyway."

"That makes it even more... more..." I can't find the words.

"More," Mona helps me out, grinning.

"Yes," I say.

We stare at each other. His hazel eyes entrance me. He's the one. He's always been the one.

"Please don't kiss in front of me," Mona says. "I may cough up blood."

That takes me out of my mood. I look at her. "Ew, Mona. How can you joke about that? Too soon."

"Thanks a lot, sis," Drake says.

"If you're going to kiss and make up, find an appropriate place. Get a room." She raises a finger. "Not mine."

"I'd love to, but we can't right now. Boulder invited us for a barbecue." He gets up. "Come on, Skye. And you, Mona, promise you won't take bullets for me anymore?"

She tilts her head at Drake. "Would *you* make that promise?"

I chuckle. "She's got you there."

"I'm the big brother. I'm supposed to take the bullet."

"Yeah, yeah. Just go kiss the witch," Mona says.

***

It's cold. We stay inside Boulder's house. Sean is manning the grill. He goes outside all the time to check when the food is done cooking. Unlike the last barbecue, this time we have only sodas and juice for drinking.

Boulder looks better. He's in a wheelchair today. He and Sean brag about who's the best cook in loud voices.

Drake and I share an alone moment. I put my hand over his. A bandage covers his hand wound, and another one covers his burnt arm. I caress him over the gauze. I wish I could transfer my Allure to him so he could heal.

"It's no big deal," Drake whispers to me. "Boulder told me chicks dig scars."

My now-again boyfriend knows how to cheer me up. "Boulder's right."

I sense two witches coming, but this time I don't fret. They're my friends.

Drake holds his cell up and shows it to Boulder. "Dude! It says here you're 'in a relationship.'"

Boulder grins.

Pri overhears and comes over. She runs her fingers through Boulder's hair in a loving gesture. "Yeah. I finally got this guy to commit."

"That's quite a feat," Drake says. "You deserve a medal."

"I already got my prize," Pri says while gazing at Boulder.

Sean opens the sliding door to the patio. "The Weird Sisters are here," he announces.

Yara is behind him and punches him in the arm. "Hey, I told you not to call us that." She comes in, followed by Greta.

They say hellos, but I spirit them away to a corner of the room.

"How are you, Greta?" I ask.

She touches the bandage over her nose. "Okay, now. Just a broken nose. Nothing that the Allure won't fix. I need to stop drinking trippy potions."

When Greta goes to grab a soda, Yara whispers, "I didn't know how to explain it to her without telling the whole story. I gave her a Forget potion and told her she had fallen facedown after she drank too much 'happy' potion." She bites her lip. "Am I a bad friend?"

"No, Yara. You're a good friend."

It's fun to have the gang together, but after we eat, Drake comes over and pulls me away.

Chapter 39: Drake

We borrowed Dad's car. I miss my battered, unreliable, ugly Volvo.

"Have you heard from London?" I ask.

"Yes. Mum, Judi, and even Elsa made my case for me. They don't have the Singularity anymore—"

"They never had her," I interrupt her.

"Good point. But we captured Miranda, Scythe, Kendall, and other Night Sisters. All of them committed crimes and broke *our* laws too. My coven is satisfied with the result."

"And you're still a witch? With a coven and everything?"

She nods. "But they won't invite me to do missions anymore. Like, ever."

"You're retired, huh?"

She chuckles.

We arrive at what I consider our place: Greenwood Park. It's still cold as always, but the sky is opening up. I can see a patch of blue, and soon the sun shines.

Like the first day we spent together, we hold hands and walk lazily on the trail around the lake.

"What are your retirement plans now?" I ask.

"I don't know. Travel. Get to know Europe."

"Really?" I didn't expect that. I was hoping that she would stay here with me. I try to hide my disappointment. "I thought you already knew Europe."

"Pfft. I know hotel rooms and fancy restaurants in big towns. I don't know the real continent. Or the people there."

"I don't understand."

"I want to backpack across Europe. Get a Eurail train pass, sleep badly, talk to strangers, not shower for a while." She looks into my eyes. "Wanna join me?"

A sense of joy invades me. This is *my* dream, the one I shared with her when we started dating. She wants to do it. And she wants to do it with me.

My smile couldn't be any broader. "Sounds like an awesome vacation. I still have some money left from the college fund."

"Let's go, then!" Skye says.

"Now?" I would go, but I'd rather take these few months until I graduate to get to know my mother.

She slaps my arm. "No, silly. In the summer. Let's finish high school and take a year off."

"Deal," I say. "But what am I going to do for college? You planted the idea in my head, remember? I don't think I can get a swimming scholarship; I missed so many meets. I'm pretty sure Coach Summers will kick me off the team."

She stops and faces me. "Well, you can do what I'm going to do. If you want to." She plays with the lapels of my jacket.

"And what's that, Queen teaser?"

"Mum knows a few people at Oxford, including the heads of department and even the Vice-Chancellor. The Sisterhood made huge donations. And, of course, we have some Sisters there. My mother always planned to get me in with a full scholarship. I bet she can get two."

What the what? "I can't, Skye."

"It's yours if you want to. Just for once, forget your pride."

"Skye…"

"Please. For me?" She bats her eyelashes playfully at me.

Her indigo blue eyes bewitch me once again. I'd follow her anywhere. "Anything for you."

She grins and kisses me. I've been yearning for that kiss for a long time.

It may be a pipe dream. I don't care. I'm with her today. I intend to be with her tomorrow.

Maybe until the end of time.

Chapter 40: Jane

The violent winds blow from the sea. Ocean Shores' beaches are almost deserted this time of the year. I'm sitting on the thick, dark gray sand while Jason flies a kite.

No one else is around. I take my sweater's hood off and enjoy the wind lashing against my face. No one here will recognize the old Jane. They would never think of looking so close to Seattle, but that's not the only strategy I'm using to hide.

Shifting is one of the Charms I stole from Mona. I can't turn into a completely different person, but my facial features have changed enough so I don't resemble Jane anymore. Of course I can't disguise my voice or my height, but at least my hair is colored a sandy blonde. It'll look even better after I let it grow a little. The Shifting made my nose, chin, and eyes smaller, and my cheekbones lower. I changed my eye color to hazel, like Drake's.

It's unsettling when I face myself in the mirror, but it's a small price to pay for freedom. And I look all right.

The menacing skies above don't scare me, nor does the promise of coming rain. Freedom. It's been a long time—years, really—since I didn't have to look over my shoulder.

I don't even have to worry about another Sister tracking my magical signature: I'm a Singularity now, and I leave no trace of energy.

Maybe I should call the Neills in Idaho just to let them know we're okay. They were our family once, after all. But we can never go back.

I take a deep drag from my cigarette.

What now? Jason and I can start over. He can recover. My little brother looks okay on the outside, but he wakes up every night with nightmares. We need a happy, safe place. An upbeat atmosphere.

My fingers dig into the coarse sand. I like this texture. Maybe a beach city. Not like this, but a sunny, vibrant place. Away from all covens. I've been moving closer and closer to the ocean: Idaho, Spokane, Seattle... but I want a warm beach. No more clouds, no more gloominess. Jason deserves more. I deserve more.

Maybe Cabo. Or Rio or Kingston. Maybe the Mediterranean Riviera.

I smile at the abundance of possibility. I've lived my life on a one-way track for a long time, going from one goal to the next, from one need to the next. Running away from some people or chasing after others.

Forget them all. Kendall and Miranda, Drake and Skye. Brianna. Cillian. They're all in the past. The only one I care about is Mona. If it weren't for her, Jason wouldn't be here right now.

He's trying to do a tough guy routine and stands in the icy surf as if it doesn't bother him. I pretend I don't notice his knees shaking, and I suppress a chuckle.

Mona. She's all right. I'd like to spend more time with her. She would be a good friend to Jason; they're about the same age.

I hope she enjoys my gift. Well, gifts.

Chapter 41: Mona

I'm back to being just a plain girl. I love it.

Being the Singularity was exhausting. Oh, yeah, and life-threatening. I'm happy that people treat me like any other girl now.

I need to figure out how I am going to work things out with Patricia. I will talk to her, but I still don't see her as my mother. Both Dad and Drake have accepted her back, not as part of the family, but as some friend of the family. I don't even know if she's going to stay here or go back into hiding. Well, one step at a time.

Someone knocks on the door. "You ready?"

"Come in, Pain," I say. "Almost. Need to brush my teeth."

She enters the room and squeezes my shoulder briefly before plopping down on the bed. She reaches for my tablet and starts swiping away.

I'm glad Pain and I cleared things up. When I told her I was flattered but I just wasn't wired that way, it was a relief for both of us. After a week of readjustment, we went back to just being best friends, BFFs, besties.

I didn't need to convince her, to manipulate her.

Back when I was with Jane, she figured out I had another Charm: Persuasion. Funny, no one besides Jane knows I have it, but Drake mentioned to me that Patricia has it too.

Only, I had it in Singularity levels. That's how I convinced Drake—and later, Dad—to let me stay with Jane. That's why Skye agreed to help rescue Jason when I asked her. It's a handy Charm to have.

But Pain moving on was not a result of me using powers on her. I'm surprised how well we handle it. Now she tells me she has a crush on a girl from her neighborhood who goes to private school. It's fun seeing it from the outside. Their flirting, their talks.

Pain is so happy right now. She looks at me from the bed. "I've got a date." Pain gives me a sheepish smile.

"What?"

"Alice and I are going to the movies. Lame, I know."

"Are. You. Kidding? This is huge! Tell me more."

Her grin spreads wide. "First, finish what you're doing. I'll tell you on the way to school. Is Drake driving us?"

"He'd better," I say. "Drake!" I yell to the house. "Wait for us!"

After a second, I hear him yelling back from downstairs, "Hurry up, dummy!"

Pain snorts. "Now that you're not the Singularity anymore, no one treats you with respect."

"I know, right?" I giggle and go into the bathroom, taking my purse with me. I lock the door.

With the Allure gone, now all I see when I look at the mirror is my old face. I'm Mona again, not the Singularity.

I have to be honest: I miss it. Being pretty, I mean.

The boys are not after me anymore. It's a relief. Now I know that the ones that are interested are attracted to the real me, not a magical, altered Barbie doll version of me. Yeah, way to kid yourself, Mona.

Well, a little make-up can't hurt. I apply a quick light base, so my face doesn't look too pale. I reach into my purse, looking for my lipstick, and my fingers brush my lighter.

I hold it at eye-level, staring at it. To the world, I'm not a witch anymore, but I'm still a Wiccan. My lighter is for candles and incense. I light it up and look mesmerized at the flickering flame.

I promised I wouldn't do it anymore, but I can't help it. I put my hand above the flame, lowering until my palm touches the top of the lighter.

Nothing. No pain.

The flame dies, and I put the lighter away. I look at my hands. They're glowing with green energy.

I lost Allure, but I kept Fire Immunity and other Charms. Like Persuasion, which will be useful if someone suspects something. And the ability to hide a magical signature.

It was a nice gift. You were fair, Jane. A fifty-fifty split is as fair as it goes.

It'll be our secret.

THE END

AUTHOR'S NOTE

Thank you for reading DARKEST FATE. If you enjoyed the book, please leave a review, even if it's just a brief paragraph, at the online ebook stores. Word of mouth is vital for an author to succeed. Your review makes a difference and would be much appreciated. Thanks!

Sign up for the newsletter ((http://bit.ly/fabiobuenoemail/) to keep up-to-date about new releases, promotions, and giveaways. Your email will never be shared, and you can unsubscribe at any time.

I love connecting with readers! Find me on my website (FabioBueno.com), Facebook (facebook.com/FabioBuenoAuthor), and Twitter (twitter.com/_FabioBueno_).

All the best,
Fabio

GLOSSARY

Charms: natural magical powers. Each Sister has two, which manifest after Daybreak. Charms are always active and cannot be "turned off" or countered with potions. Most Sisters have an Allure Charm. Other common ones are Athletics, Intellect, Charisma, and Trust.

Coven: a gathering of Sisters. A witch's coven is a second family to her.

Craft: the culture of the witches. It includes their values, traditions, history, and system of beliefs. Magic is but a part of the Craft.

Daybreak: the coming-of-age of a Sister. A Sister's personal magic awakens at Daybreak, around her fifteenth birthday, usually accompanied by a small burst of magical energy.

Goddess: most Sisters believe the Goddess is a deity, but some view the Goddess as a symbol, an icon, or a manifestation of magical energy. Irrespective of belief, all Sisters pray to the Goddess.

Knowing: somebody who knows magic exists, but is not a witch herself.

Magic/Personal Magic/Magical Energy: all living things possess this universal energy, but only witches can tap into it, connect with the Goddess, and create potions and spells.

Night Magic: Night magic, Night coven, and Night Sisters are the twisted versions of the true Craft. Night magic is more powerful than regular magic.

Potions: brewed during rituals and infused with a Sister's personal magic. Require specific ingredients. Popular potions are Fancy Me, Sleep, and Truth. The most common methods of delivery are beverages, oils, serums, and ointments.

Rituals: solo ceremonies performed by Sisters, with the goal of meditation, connecting with the Goddess, and creating spells and potions. A ritual performed by more than one witch is called a commune ritual.

Singularity: the most powerful witch alive. Her reserve of magical energy is exponentially higher than a regular witch's. The Singularity has more than two Charms, and only releases energy when she casts a spell or loses control of her magic.

Spells: prayers and incantations recited during a ritual where the Sister embeds a little of her personal magic into the prayer. Prayers usually require a simple offering to the Goddess and involve burning of herbs, leaves, flowers, oils, or incense.

Talisman/Amulet: a small object imbued with personal magic; a vessel for a spell or potion.

Veil: an unwritten code, followed by all magic users: nobody reveals the existence of magic. It's the Craft's most important rule.

Witch/Sister: a practitioner of the Craft.

Witch Sense: all Sisters release a constant flow of magical energy that can be felt by other Sisters nearby.

ACKNOWLEDGMENTS

When I started this journey, I had no idea I would connect with so many people. Writing is a pleasure, but meeting and bonding with wonderful friends made this endeavor even more rewarding.

Here are my imperfect and incomplete, yet heartfelt, thank-yous.

My critique group, Writers in The Rain: Brenda Beem, Martina Dalton, Angela Orlowski-Peart, Eileen Riccio, and Suma Subramaniam. You made me a better person and a better writer.

DMs, SCBWI, YA Ninjas, WANAs, Club Indie, and WG2E Street Team. Your presence is virtual; your influence is real.

The League of Awesome Pros: Alyssa Linn Palmer (Black Belt Editor), Amanda Shofner (Jedi Proofreader), and Martina Dalton (Ninja Cover Designer).

My unofficial mentors: C. C. Mackenzie, Jillian Dodd, Rhonda Hopkins, and Diane Capri.

Friends who supported me all the way (and even beta-read sometimes): Cindy, Julie, Claudio, Carlos, Flavia, Andreas, Jose, and Lucio.

My family and my in-laws. You always believed.

My kids. Each day, I thank the skies for being part of your lives.

Wonder Wife. Forever my sweetheart.

ABOUT THE AUTHOR

Fabio resides in the Pacific Northwest with his wife and kids. When not writing or reading, he geeks out with family and friends, solidifies his reputation as the world's slowest runner, and acts very snobbish about movies. He loves to hear from readers and hangs out here:

@_FabioBueno_

Fabiobueno.com

Facebook.com/FabioBuenoAuthor

www.ingramcontent.com/pod-product-compliance
Lightning Source LLC
Chambersburg PA
CBHW070915180626

46817CB00003B/1076